Embrace

Embrace

Megan Derr

Embrace
By Megan Derr

Published by Less Than Three Press

Edited by Drowning London
Cover art by Imagining Designs

Electronic Edition October 2009

Printed in the United States of America

ISBN 978-1-936202-03-4

Table of Contents

Lobelia

(prologue)

Aubrey squealed happily as mama gave him another bilberry, popping it into his mouth and chewing enthusiastically, thanking her with a smile, displaying lips and teeth that had been stained blue from the berry juice.

Mama smiled back, pretty and delicate, smelling like flowers and cake. Next to her, Mina hummed one of her lullabies.

He held out his hand for another berry. "Please, mama?"

"One more," Mama said, holding up one finger to make certain he understood.

Aubrey nodded, and with another thanks, pushed the last berry into his mouth, clapping his hands in glee.

Berries eaten, he picked up the flowers they had bought for sissy. She was sick again, and had not been able to go with him and mama and Mina, so they had bought her flowers. "What called?" he asked.

"Lobelia," Mina said.

"Bee-yah," Aubrey repeated dutifully. "Smell pretty."

"Yes, they do," Mama replied, smiling and reaching out to touch the flowers lightly, then moving to brush back a floppy curl from Aubrey's forehead. "Sissy will like them very much."

Aubrey nodded, and looked again at the basket of pretty purple flowers. He couldn't wait to show her, and then they could help Mama and Mina put them in the garden. He liked playing in the garden, digging holes and pulling up bad flowers.

The carriage bounced and jerked and rumbled beneath them, making him knock back and forth between Mina and Mama, but Aubrey didn't mind. Soon they would be home and he could give the flowers to Sissy and show Daddy what else they got in town and then they could have dinner and maybe Daddy would let him have more wine like a Big Person.

He almost fell over when the carriage abruptly stopped, but Mina caught him and held him tight.

Strange voices came from outside the carriage, and he thought he heard them say Mama's name, but it didn't sound like Daddy's voice, and he and Mina were the only ones that called Mama by her name.

"Stay here, sweetheart," Mama said, and kissed his brow.

"Don't go, Mama," Aubrey said, letting go of the flowers to grip Mama's skirts, cause she only called him that when Something Bad was going to happen. "Stay."

"Shh, sweetheart. Mama and Mina are just going to talk to some friends, all right? She'll be right back." With that, she pushed open the carriage door and vanished outside, Mina following right behind her.

Aubrey stayed inside, drawing up his legs and holding them against his chest.

He let go to cover his ears as a lot of shouting and screaming and other scary sounds started up, tears rolling down his cheeks cause this was Bad and he wanted Daddy cause Daddy always made scary stuff not be scary anymore.

Then the sounds stopped, and then he heard a lot of noises that he knew belonged to horses.

He waited for Mama and Mina to come back.

When a long, long time passed and they didn't come, he slowly pushed the door open and cried "Mama!" like he always did when a monster snuck under his bed and he needed her to scare it away. She always came in her nightdress and holding a candle and got down and yelled at the monsters.

Only she didn't come this time.

Sniffling, wiping at his yucky nose, Brey bent down and slowly climbed down from the carriage. Without help, it was hard, cause the carriage was high, high off the ground and the steps were for Big People, not him.

He slipped and fell, landing in the dirt of the path. Scrambling to his feet, he looked around anxiously for Mama, but it was getting dark and was hard to see and—

Oh, there she was. Sleeping? Why was mommy sleeping? Mina was sleeping too...

He ran over to them, and dropped down next to Mama, putting his hands on her to shake her awake like he sometimes had to do in the morning when she didn't get up right away.

Only his hands came away wet, and he wondered if Mama had spilled something. It was dark, but he kinda thought it looked like something red. Frowning, he went back to shaking Mama, but she never woke up.

It was really really dark when he heard more horses coming, and when he turned he saw lanterns swinging in the dark – then Daddy's voice broke through, and suddenly the dark and Mama and Mina sleeping wasn't as scary.

"Daddy! Daddy!"

"Brey!" Daddy's voice growled in the dark, and he almost thought for a moment that Daddy sounded scared, but that was impossible because Daddy wasn't scared of anything.

Then Daddy was picking him up, and Aubrey hugged him tight. "Daddy, Mama is sleeping and won't wake up."

"I know, Brey," Daddy said, and his voice sounded funny, almost like Daddy was crying, but Daddy didn't cry. "Come on, Brey, let's get you home."

"Mama? Mina?"

But Daddy didn't answer, even when Aubrey kept asking, which made Aubrey start crying again and he wanted Mama and Mina to wake up and to be home in bed or playing in the garden.

He cried and cried, all the way home, until Nurse showed up and took him and told him to drink from his little cup and Aubrey suddenly felt tired and only remembered Nurse picking him up again and heading for the stairs

Forget Me Not

(chapter one)

Aubrey shivered and drew his cloak more tightly around his shoulders, tugging the fur-lined hood up just a bit more, wishing home was not still an hour or so away.

He could, of course, simply use the carriage – but he'd much rather freeze to death, which he was quite nicely proving.

The wind picked up, making him grimace, but after three days of travel, one hour more would not kill him. Not unless the snow resumed falling, but thankfully the sky seemed to clear for that to happen anytime soon.

Sighing softly, he twisted around to examine the carriage behind, which was packed with the majority of his things. The rest would follow by wagon more slowly, mostly a few small pieces of furniture and crates of books, warm-weather clothing and other things he would not need right away. Those things he did require, or simply refused to be without, were packed into the carriage.

Including the dog rose he was bringing his sister, snitched from the school greenhouse. He didn't think she had a dog rose yet, though she very nearly had every rose known to the world and a few unique to the Sangre gardens.

He frowned, thinking of the home he had not seen in five years. His father, Lord Karl Bathory, Earl of Sangre, had not been pleased when his son and heir had decided to depart to follow his studies, rather than remain at home to focus upon the family estate.

His sister had been rather unhappy as well, though she at least had been understanding and forgiving. Still, he did wonder at his reception. He'd sent word ahead that he was returning, but received not so much as a single note in reply.

It made him nervous, even as it did not surprise him.

Sighing again, he took out his pocket watch and flipped it open, staring at the minute family portrait painted with meticulous care. It was old, a copy of the family portrait which had once hung in the grand salon, now buried away in the attic somewhere per his father's instructions. It was of his parents, himself at age four, and his sister at two.

Not quite two years after the portrait had been painted and hung, his mother and her Pet had been brutally murdered by bandits while returning from a trip to the little village near their family seat. He had, apparently, been with them. Aubrey did not recall it.

His father had often said that his lingering fear of being inside carriages came from that night.

To Aubrey's mind, it was also when his family had ceased to be one. He had vague memories of a much warmer father, though they were fuzzy and, he felt, probably all made up. The servants had told him stories of his parents, how warm and loving they had been, but he had never been able to match the stories to the cold man who spent all his time locked away in his bedroom or study, emerging only to find fault with someone and administer suitable punishment.

He wondered what his reception would be, if there would be any sort of reception at all, or if he would merely see his father over the dinner table as though not a day had passed from the moment of his leaving.

Was Carmilla all right? He had written her often, as well as Stregoni, but both had been annoyingly vague on the matter of her condition. Not wanting him to worry, likely, but all it did was make him worry that much more.

He thought again of the dog rose, it's vibrant pink petals, and hoped it was secured well against the biting cold.

The sharp tinkling of jingle bells drew him from his brooding, and he looked up as he came round the bend in the road – and broke into a smile as he saw who was ahead of him.

No matter how many years might pass, there would never be any mistaken the vibrant, chaotic mass of orange-red curls of Stregoni Benefici.

"Hail, stranger," he said cheerfully, shoving back his hood so he was visible. He laughed when Stregoni whipped around, the blue-gray eyes going wide.

"Brey!" Stregoni explained. "Well, I never! No one told me you were due to arrive. That brat Carmilla, she probably wanted to surprise me."

Aubrey attempted to smooth down his messy, light brown hair, moss green eyes meeting Stregoni's as they drew even. "No doubt, knowing Milla," Aubrey said with a smile. "So tell me everything, Stregoni. What have I missed? How is my sister? Father? My damned cousin."

Stregoni's face abruptly clouded, pain flashing through his eyes, before he smiled through it and recovered his levity. His fingers reached up to touch the pin nestled in his neck cloth, a beautiful enameled pink rose. It stood out bright against the dark cream stock, a lovely compliment to the deep forest green of his coat and the black winter cloak. "Your sister is doing relatively well, all things considered. I have put her on a new medicine, and I go today to see how it has performed this past week, see what adjustments might be made. Your father is your father," Stregoni said with a shrug. "Your cousin..." He grimaced, and again touched the rose at his throat. "Gille only grows worse with every passing year, I swear."

"I cannot say it surprises me," Aubrey said with a sigh. He had managed mostly to forget about his damned cousin.

Just days after his twelfth birthday, his cousin Gille had come to live with them. Why, no ever said. To this day, Aubrey did not know. So far as he knew, Uncle George was alive and quite healthy, though he had always been an odd recluse who never left his own estate.

Perhaps he was too much of a recluse to tend his own son; Aubrey simply did not know. Nor did he really care, as Gille had always been a brat with a bit of a mean streak, who strove to ensure he made no real sense to anyone.

Of the family, he was the only one who bothered to move about society, travel to the city every other Season or so – and if he wanted to travel, Aubrey's father certainly took no issue. It was only Aubrey's freedom to do as he pleased that Lord Sangre curtailed as best he could.

Scowling, Aubrey switched the direction of his thoughts. "Is there anything about which I should be warned?"

Stregoni winced. "Actually, there is – and it did not make sense to me until I saw, and now I'm afraid it is all too clear."

Aubrey groaned. "What?"

"Gille left two weeks ago on a trip for which he would not give details. Not unusual – but he returned yesterday with a new Pet, and said only it was not for him, but a present for 'someone special'. I should have known he was being an ass, but he sounded so sincere..."

Once again pain flickered across Stregoni's face, and Aubrey wondered at it, but it was gone so quickly he half wondered if he was imagining it. Even if he was not, he sensed Stregoni would not explain it.

Then Stregoni's words actually struck him. "A Pet?" he echoed. "Never say they have purchased a Pet for me."

"I think they have," Stregoni said, voice sympathetic. "Most would consider it a marvelous gift." He paused, then spoke again more hesitantly. "He's quite handsome..."

Aubrey grimaced. "I don't care if he's the most beautiful man on the face of the planet, I do not want a Pet." His mouth tightened at the thought of being saddled with a Pet. Not that he had any right to complain – as Stregoni had said, most would consider a Pet a fine gift indeed. Knowing his father, no expense had been spared in the acquisition, and while there was much fault to find with Gille, his sense of taste was not one of them.

No doubt the Pet was quite up to Aubrey's tastes, though how his father and Gille had known his tastes in such matters, he shuddered to think about.

Still, he had never liked the concept of Pets.

Pets hailed from a small country far to the south, originally. A strange race of human-like creatures that did not need food as did ordinary beasts and men, but blood. Human blood was best of all, though until they were sold they survived on animal blood.

This was because once a Pet fed on the blood of his owner, he ceased being able to drink any other form of blood. His body would no longer digest it properly. Once this new Pet drank Aubrey's blood, he would be required to feed on Aubrey or die of starvation.

Aubrey hated it.

Though they were bred and raised across the world now, the finest Pets still came from the small country of their origin, where they had long ago been subjugated and enslaved by the humans there. Kept as Pets in their native homeland, after the blood dependency quirk was discovered, the popularity of it had slowly spread across the world.

Any nobleman worth anything had a Pet.

His mother had possessed a Pet. His father had one now, a pale-skinned beauty named Elisabeth. Gille had one, a younger man. Handsome, as Aubrey recalled, too severe to be truly beautiful. Black hair, with strange eyes the same shade of purple as monkshood. Not an eye color found on any human, which was why it stuck in Aubrey's memory. Francois, was his name. Aubrey had never liked him.

"I suppose it's far too late to turn around and say I'm not returning after all," he said with a sigh.

"Too late," Stregoni agreed cheerfully. "You are the ally which I have sorely needed, and I am not letting you out of my sight again for a very long time. That aside," he continued more seriously, "your sister could use some more company. She swears she gets along quite well with Gille and your father, but I know you would do her far better than any tonic."

Aubrey nodded, putting his anger away to deal with later. He was glad to be home, he was – he just wished that there were not already matters cropping up to sour it. "I still do not want a Pet."

"Well, make the best of it," Stregoni said peaceably. "Unless you can somehow manage to talk him out of it, your father had settled the matter. Perhaps the new Pet will become a friend, that happens more often than anyone cares to admit."

"I suppose," Aubrey said, shrugging the words off. "Tell me about yourself, Stregoni. How is the business? Your mother? Discover anything new? Acquire some new patients?" He winked. "A lover?"

Stregoni looked away, shrugging in his turn. "No lover," he said tersely. "A few new patients, though the kind that want an easy remedy to everything. That Marquis that lives a day or so from here has requested my services for his child a few times now, though I'm afraid he has a breathing problem that is not curable. Still, I try." He smiled as he turned back. "Thanks to your sister, I have access to the best herbs and flowers in the country."

Aubrey returned the smile. "That is Milla; I'm sure it makes her happy to help where she can." He sighed softly. "So nothing has been discovered as to her illness?"

"No, Brey, and I'm sorry for it. She simply seems to have been born with a weak body. I think it is her heart, but cannot say for certain." Stregoni spread his hands in frustration. "I will never stop trying, but..."

"I know, Stregoni," Aubrey said, taking one leather-clad hand in his own. "It wasn't an accusation."

Stregoni squeezed his hand, then let it go. "Come on, we're nearly home, and you can see for yourself that she is as fit as she can possibly be – and probably in her prettiest dress, because her big brother is coming home."

Aubrey smiled, and pulled up the hood of his cloak once more before chasing after Stregoni, who had bolted ahead, laughing as their horses raced down the path.

They stopped before a house that was probably the oldest in the region, and had belonged to the Bathory family had first been granted the Sangre title.

Sangre Manor was beautiful but somber, a house built of dark stone, settled deep into the thick forest that consumed much of the region. The stone was of deepest gray, holding a faint gleam when the sun struck it properly, looking like something out of a penny-dreadful when the moon was bright. Deep blue shutters and a like door, with dark marble steps leading up to it.

Far to the right, near the small pond filled with white and orange fish, was the stone bench half-buried by a weeping willow where he had so often sat as a child.

Further beyond that was the footpath into the forest where had often 'run away' before dark and fear forced him back, to try again another day.

On other side of the house extended part of the greenhouse, an undertaking which was nearly as large as the house itself, boasting a garden that was vibrant no matter the time of year, always warm and friendly, and the only one of its kind in all the country – possibly all the world, though Aubrey did not know for certain.

He knew only that it made his sister happy, that she loved it as much as their mother once had – according to various sources, anyway.

As they drew up to the house, the front door flew open and a whole gaggle of people came spilling out – servants to the last, and with a sharp words from the head butler, they all lined up neatly.

Dismounting, Aubrey moved to address them, but before he could say a word more figures stepped out of the house, and the words caught in his throat with nervousness.

His father had aged five years, but as always he aged with dignity and grace. His hair was mostly gray, now, but much of the light brown exactly like his own still remained. His eyes were light blue, and age had not diminished their sharpness. Unlike Aubrey, he stood tall.

The only person as tall as his father was his cousin Gille, whose mouth was curved in a smirk that Aubrey had not forgotten in his absence. Gille seemed unable to shape his mouth in any other way. Of course, it could be because the smirk rather suited his cool beauty. Gille was everything Aubrey was not – tall where Aubrey was short, fashionably sparse where Aubrey just avoided being stocky, stunning where Aubrey had turned out merely ordinary.

Like Aubrey and his father, Gille had light brown hair. He wore it long, however, and like now it was most often braided, tied with a ribbon. His clothes were the very first of fashion, and like Stregoni his cravat pin took the shape of a flower – a red peony. They were a strange contrast with his jade green eyes, the bold and delicate colors clashing...and yet on Gille, it somehow worked.

"Father," he greeted slowly, hesitating.

"Aubrey, it is good you are home," his father said quietly, voice as level as it ever was, giving nothing away. There was no way to tell if he meant the words, or how he meant them.

Before he could say something, likely something he would regret, a last figure appeared in the doorway. She was the spitting image of their father, but with all the feminine touches. Only the fact she was weak and sickly kept Carmilla Bathory from being a true beauty of society. She would be a diamond of the first water, if only she were healthy.

He moved quickly up the steps to embrace her, kiss her cheek. "Milla, it is good to see you again."

"Brey, you're home," Carmilla said, kissing his cheeks, squeezing him tightly. "It's so good to see you again."

He hugged her again, and held fast as he turned to greet the servants and accept their expression of excitement and pleasure at his return. Finally he faced his father and Gille again.

"Cousin," Gille said, still smirking. "I see you brought the good doctor with you." His eyes slid briefly to Stregoni, standing silent nearby, then slid back to Aubrey. "We have a gift for you."

"So I heard," Aubrey said. "I do not want him."

"One does not refuse gifts," his father replied, face and tone implacable, but somehow Aubrey knew the matter was over before it had begun. He would accept the Pet, and that was that.

Stifling an urge to mount his horse and ride off back to school, he allowed Carmilla to lead him into the house.

Inside, it had scarcely changed at all. The paintings, the marble floor and costly rugs, the crystal hanging from the ceiling...little things were gone, replaced by others, but the overall affect was as though he had not been gone more than an afternoon.

Nearby stood two men and a woman.

The woman was his father's Pet, the pale and beautiful Elisabeth. Aubrey had rarely spoken to her growing up, though she was always kind when they did cross paths. She rarely left the suite of rooms that belonged to his father, and usually did so only at his father's bidding.

On her left stood Francois, as beautiful and creepy as Aubrey remembered. He did not spare that Pet a glance, though he felt the cold chill of purple eyes upon him.

His full attention, however, was quickly stolen by the one Pet he did not recognize – his Pet.

Beside him, Carmilla murmured something, but Aubrey did not catch the words.

The Pet was beautiful, there was no denying that. He did not have Gille's cold, dark beauty though...no, he was all warm tones and colors. Tall, but next to Aubrey everyone was tall really. Still – he would not come up past the Pet's shoulder.

His hair was the color of beeswax, cropped extremely short and seemingly fine, delicate whisps of it clinging to his cheeks and forehead. The skin was smooth and flawless, and ever so faintly sunkissed, lending a further impression of warmth.

By stark contrast, his eyes were so dark Aubrey could not tell their color. He was also dressed head to foot in black. Severe, but he wore it well. The oddest thing about his appearance was that he wore no neck cloth. Instead, a startling amount of skin was bare, the worst of it covered up only by what Aubrey realized was a collar – a popular affectation inflicted upon Pets.

Perhaps in jest, affixed to the black leather collar as a cravat pin. Flowers must be in fashion, for like Stregoni and Gille, the Pet's pin was in the shape of a flower – a vibrant, beautiful forget-me-not.

The Pet stepped forward, and sketched a deep, elegant bow, not quite rising as he lifted his head to look at Aubrey.

Event his close, he could not tell the color of the Pet's eyes. They looked almost black, except he could see the pupil's quite clearly.

Aubrey realized he wasn't breathing. Shaking himself, he stepped forward.

"Master," the Pet murmured.

"What is your name?" Aubrey asked. If he was going to have a Pet, then he may as well accept it with dignity. He had learned the hard and painful way that making a scene only hurt himself.

The Pet smiled faintly. "Ruthven, Master."

"Ruthven," Aubrey repeated. "You must already know I am Aubrey."

"Yes, Master."

Aubrey nodded, and extended his right arm, wrist up. "Welcome, then."

"I thank you, Master," Ruthven murmured, and for a moment something hot and bright flared in his dark eyes. It made Aubrey shiver, though he could not put a name to what it was he had seen.

Then his wrist was taken up in one gloved hand, the black satin warm against his frozen skin. He shivered again as he caught a hint of the long, sharp fangs, and bit back a cry of pain as they sank into his skin.

It was the strangest sensation, and not one to which he would ever grow accustomed. Only humans, he thought, would decide it was fashionable to have their blood sucked.

As easy that, he was responsible for the life of another. If he died, so too would Ruthven. He stood immobile as Ruthven finally rose to his full height, licking blood from his lips. What was he supposed to say or do now?

"Thank you, father," he said stiffly after the silence stretched on.

"Gille picked him out," Sangre replied, coming up to stand beside Aubrey, eyes on Ruthven. "He is lovely. Suitable?" He asked the question, but it was clearly rhetorical.

Aubrey nodded in reply anyway. He looked at Gille, but did not offer any thanks. From the expression on Gille's face, he had not expected any.

A bell rang, and Sangre held an arm out to Elisabeth. "Come, dinner is ready. We will eat as a proper family for the first time in too long."

It was a rebuke, as well as a tacit order that Aubrey would not be permitted to leave home again.

"Home, sweet home," Aubrey muttered to himself, then gave Carmilla his arm and followed his father to the dining room.

Love Lies Bleeding

(chapter two)

Stregoni had always been an insomniac, a trait he had acquired from his mother. So many nights they had sat up together, grateful at least not to be alone in their sleeplessness, both envying those who could sleep effortlessly through the night – including his father, who slept like the dead.

He hated it, not least of all because he always did incredibly stupid things when left alone in the dark of night.

Like wander the halls, hoping and dreading that someone else might be awake.

Do you want me?

He balled his hands into fists, and tried to convince himself he should go back to his room and resume work annotating his *Pharmacopoeia.* But brandy settled warm in his belly, buzzing in his head, and he could not stand still.

The halls were empty as he wandered them, his every step a thundering echo on marble tile, mercifully muffled whenever he trod over rug.

Go back to bed, idiot, he tried to tell himself. He didn't know why he'd bothered, it had been a lost cause from the moment he'd left his own home to stay at the Sangre estate for a few days.

As he reached the east wing, music filtered toward him. Piano, the music a slow, heartbreaking piece. A thousand times he'd wanted to ask why it was always sad music, why nothing happy ever came out of that piano, but it was one in a thousand questions he never managed to voice.

Because like the ones he did dare voice, it would only met with some cold, cruel reply.

He was always cruel, had been from the first, but Stregoni had never been able to walk away, and stay away.

Why do you always act so cool, doctor? Do you think you're deceiving me? Your eyes are blue fire, when you look at me. Do you want me?

Like the proverbial moth to the flame, Stregoni wandered down the hall the music room. Their eyes had met for only a moment over dinner, but it had been enough to let him know that they both would be drunk tonight.

He pushed the door open, and tried one last time to remind himself of all the reasons this was a bad idea. It had never worked before, not since that first night, and it would not work this time.

All manner of potions and tonics and syrups cluttered the shelves of his apothecary in town. He knew the recipes for more medicines than he could count – and nearly all of them could also be considered deadly poisons.

None of them was as potent or addictive or potentially fatal as what drew him time and again to the cruel embrace of the beautiful man playing a mournful song on the piano.

Gille was the very definition of breathtaking, especially now when there was no one around to look down upon or impress, no social engagements pending, no visitors looming. No, he was dressed only in black breeches and a white shirt he had not bothered to lace, his long hair loose around his shoulders, hiding the elegant lines of his face and the bewitching gold-flecked pale green eyes.

Stregoni hovered in the doorway, part of him knowing he should flee, the rest of him too addicted to even think of it.

The music room was a somber place, the floor all black marble tile, the paneling a deep, rich red. Silver candelabra were scattered about, though only the one nearest the piano was actually lit.

Just behind Gille was a massive portrait of two men. It looked as though someone had simply painted Aubrey twice, but it was in fact Karl and George Bathory, the respective fathers of Aubrey and Gille. Twin brothers, and Stregoni recalled his father saying they had once been quite close. Though George Bathory lived only a few miles away, in a nearby estate, Stregoni had never met him. The man had become a recluse since the death of his wife in childbirth.

So much of a recluse, in fact, that Gille had come to live with his uncle. Beyond that, Stregoni knew nothing about the situation. No one knew anything, except Gille and Lord Sangre.

All Stregoni knew was that Gille could be and often was cold and cruel, and that he never got kinder than merely condescending.

Except sometimes...

He shook his head and looked again at the portrait. Gille had much in common with the twins, much in common with Aubrey, but there was a beauty to his features that they lacked, and that had likely come from his mother.

The two men were only in their mid-twenties at the time of the portrait. Handsome, severe, hinting at the over strict Lord of the manor Lord Sangre would eventually become – though, at that, Stregoni could not tell which was which.

One was seated, hands clasped over one knee, as though he were listening attentively to an unseen speaker. The second twin stood over the seat, slightly bent, as if to whisper to his brother when the speaker turned away for a moment. The chair was black velvet, matching their dark clothes, cuffs and throats displaying lace that was almost garishly white by contrast. To the right of the chair was a marble planter, from which tumbled the long, deep red blossoms of the flower Stregoni knew was called love-lies-bleeding.

He was stirred from his musings by the sudden absence of music, and dropped his gaze to see that Gille had turned to look at him.

The green eyes drew him like an opium addict to laudanum.

"The midnight hour strikes, and the doctor appears. Some would say that makes you a witch, doctor," Gille said, mouth curving in that too familiar smirk. Stregoni ached to wipe it from his face. Permanently. He wanted to see something tender, something...

Shoving the pointless, dangerous thoughts aside, he drew just close enough that he could reach out and touch if he wanted. Instead, he waited.

Gille reached out to pick up the glass of wine perched on the edge of the piano. Deep, blood red, and probably dry – Gille had always favored dry wines. His fingers were long, elegant, the nails meticulously manicured. He took a deep sip, eyes never leaving Stregoni's, the fine gold-flecked jade color only dulled a bit by the undoubtedly potent wine.

The sound of the glass clinking as Gille set it down again seemed shockingly loud in the ringing silence.

Brandy burned deep in his gut, but Gille burned hotter still throughout his entire body.

A wicked addiction he would do best to rid himself of, but he was as hopeless as the addicts he tried to help every week.

Gille touched him first, and Stregoni counted it a small, cheap victory. He was no better dressed than Gille, wearing only the bare minimum required to preserve modesty until he reached the music room.

He shivered faintly as his shirt was pushed off his shoulders, the laces teasing briefly across his nipples before Gille's mouth and tongue trailed with agonizing slowness across his stomach. Reaching out, he shoved his hands beneath Gille's shirt, digging his nails into the soft skin beneath, feeling hard muscle. A spoiled brat Gille might be, but he was too vain and proud to allow his body to spoil.

Lowering his head, he breathed in the scents that clung to Gille, remnants of his soap – cypress and marigold, and a hint of cologne which remained elusive. He moaned softly as Gille's mouth moved higher, leaving a trail of tingling heat, making him gasp sharply and tighten his hold until he earned a noise in return.

Gille abruptly stood up, arms bands around Stregoni's waist. Standing at his full height, he was at least a head taller than Stregoni. He nipped at Gille's collar bone, but before he could get a better taste of the fine skin, his head was tilted up and his mouth plundered.

He tasted like his dark, dry wine, a hint of clove. Something darker still and so rich, something that was all Gille. If he could distill it, whatever it was about Gille that drugged him so, he could addict the world to it.

His mouth was explored, devoured, taken until not a breath remained in his body, and he was left dizzy and gasping. Only then did he realize they had moved across the room to the black velvet chaise lounge.

Gille grabbed his shirt and removed it entirely, then removed his own, before those graceful fingers moved greedily to his breeches. Stregoni gasped as the cool air struck him, but almost immediately the chill was banished by Gille's fevered touch.

An addict he might be, but he was not so consumed by this wicked drug he would stand stupefied. Recovering himself some small measure, he shoved hard, sending Gille tumbling down on the chaise. Straddling him, Stregoni attacked Gille's pants, getting them open despite the delicious distraction of being yanked down to be intoxicated by another of those devastating kisses.

The kisses hurt more than anything, because at times they seemed to say things he knew Gille would never say. These nights were dirty secrets, and he still did not know why they had succumbed to that first, long ago urge one blizzard-shrouded night.

Touch after agonizing touch, gasps and moans and muffled cries, hot, sweat-slick skin, all melted into a haze of lust and need, until the fingers buried deep inside him finally slid away and he was guided down on Gille's cock, shaking hard as he adjusted to the fullness, wishing he did not miss it, need it. Hating himself for it, but unable to deny it.

Hands braced on Gille's chest, pale green eyes searing him with the wine-soaked lust that filled them, Stregoni began to move – there was nothing slow or hesitant, they were both too drugged on the moment for that. He buried his shout in Gille's mouth only just in time.

Their panting filled the music room as the fever slowly cooled, and Stregoni dreaded the return of his senses.

It came all too soon, as Gille slid from his body and the fire in his eyes cooled, then finally died.

He did not wait for the snide comments, the cruel remarks, but slid away and picked up his discarded clothes, cheeks burning with shame as he dressed.

Gille said nothing, but he could feel the cold eyes upon him, knew the cutting words hovered on the precipice, that they would tip from the sharp tongue with the next breath.

Though he knew he was no whore, at the end of these damned interludes, he felt it.

Still Gille said nothing. That was strange enough that the pace of Stregoni's heart began to increase, a flush of hope causing his steps to slow as he reached the door, and he braced a hand on the frame to turn around and see if just maybe...

"Good night, Carrot."

Cold. Dismissive. As though Gille were bored again, now that the amusement had come and gone. And that damned name. Carrot. Stregoni knew his hair was ugly, ridiculous, not the more vibrant red-gold that his mother possessed. Gille always knew where and how to hit for maximum pain with minimal effort.

He continued walking, though his steps were still slow. As he reached the end of the hallway, the sounds of slow, sad music reached his ears.

Stregoni pressed the heels of his hands to his eyes, and told himself it was the late hour, and the candlelight, which made them sting and water.

Peach Blossom

(chapter three)

Aubrey had about had enough of foul tempers.

Well, Millie he could not blame. She was tired, and her illness had taken a turn, so she was permitted to be a bit off. Father was as sours as he always was when the weather was foul. Aubrey had not expected cheerful conversation from that corner, at any rate.

Gille was ever nastier than Aubrey could ever remember him being.

Even Stregoni, upon whom he'd been counting for happy companionship, was in a foul mood.

He could not escape outside, the weather was a breath away from being a proper blizzard. Feeling very much sour himself, now, Aubrey trolled the house looking for something to either soothe his ill-temper, or something on which he could vent it.

When his hunt proved in vain, he retreated at last to the small room he had taken over as his private study and office.

He startled upon entering, as he realized someone else was in the room.

Since returning home a week ago, Aubrey had done his best to avoid Ruthven for all but the necessary feedings. Of course, Ruthven slept in his bed. Much to his regret, Aubrey had seen no way out of that particular problem.

Elisabeth and Francois both slept with their respective owners. It would be humiliating in the extreme for Ruthven if Aubrey were to make him sleep above stairs in the servant quarters like he was common help. Neither could he simply give Ruthven a room of his own – his father would put his foot right down on such an outlandish notion.

Currently, Ruthven was ensconced in the window seat, the main reason Aubrey had stolen this room away to be his own. It was wide and long, and gave a beautiful view of the west side of the house, the lush lawn and the forest beyond it.

At the edge of that forest were the faded remains of a path which Aubrey knew led straight to the house of his Uncle – Gille's father – but he had never visited his Uncle, except perhaps when he was too small to recall.

There were other paths, even more faded than the one made by brothers who had once been close, but he'd never been inclined to explore. Something about the forest nagged at him, prickled the same way being locked in a carriage bothered him.

Thoughts of the forest, however, were distant.

Ruthven had made himself quite comfortable, propped on pillows that also served to separate him from the cold glass. He was wrapped in a blanket, and had a book set in his lap. Some heavy tome that looked familiar, but which he could not at the moment place. There was very little light coming from the window, all of it blocked by piles upon piles of snow, the wind whipping up even more flakes and tossing them about.

All the reading light came instead from the various lamps Ruthven had lit, one pulled near the window that he could better see to read there. It made his beeswax hair a rich gold, warmed the sun-kissed skin.

He turned the pages with his left hand, the faintest of smiles curving his pale pink lips. Aubrey noted this only because in his right hand, Ruthven held a teacup – one from the winter set, pale green porcelain decorated with mistletoe.

"Pets drink tea?"

Ruthven looked up, then smiled and closed his book, setting his teacup aside. "It doesn't help us, but it doesn't hurt, either. I like tea."

Aubrey frowned. He did not know much about Pets, because he hated the whole idea and so avoided the matter...but he was fairly certain the breeding grounds and the Pet houses did not feed the Pets anything but blood. "Where did you drink tea?"

"Here and there," Ruthven said, head dipping, eyelids falling so long lashes just brushed his cheeks. Then he brought his gaze up to directly meet Aubrey's. "Mostly during interviews. It is rude not to drink, is it not?"

Drat it, he still could not tell the color of Ruthven's eyes. Why did it bother him so much?

Something else suddenly occurred to him. "You can read."

Ruthven's mouth quirked. "Yes, master."

Aubrey scowled. "My name is Aubrey."

"Yes, master," Ruthven said again, doing that thing with his lashes. A demure move, submissive. Yet something prickled along Aubrey's skin that said submissive and Ruthven did not belong in the same breath.

He was a Pet, though. A blood drinker bound to Aubrey for the rest of his life. If there was any life more submissive than that, Aubrey did not want to know about it.

Why was he even thinking about such things?

"How is it you are able to read? That is expressly forbidden to Pets."

Ruthven smiled. "I was...I guess you could say, my upbringing was a bit more loose than it should have been. The woman who raised me in the nursery, until I was sent off for lessons, indulged me overmuch." He dipped his head and looked up through his lashes, the very pictures of subservient and eager to oblige. "If it bothers my master, then of course I shall cease at once."

Aubrey frowned.

It was one of the top rules of Pets – they were taught all the basics of moving in polite society, but nothing that might encourage them to be dissatisfied with their lot. Keeping Pets that drank blood was much like playing with fire, even if controlling them was long ago turned into a fine art

They were not allowed to read or write. Before being sold, Pets were rendered unable to breed. They did not converse with Pets outside their own household unless given permission and strictly supervised, and even within the household the Pets did not spend overmuch time together. Scores of rules existed, for the good of everyone involved, or so the supporters said.

"What are you reading?" he asked finally. If he was going to be saddled with a Pet, why not one who broke a few rules? At least Ruthven seemed to be in a good mood.

Ruthven lifted the book so he could see the cover.

"What do you think of it?" Aubrey asked, almost smacking himself for not recognizing it. A philosophical volume; not one of his favorites, but a compelling one. He stepped closer despite himself, already eager for the chance at conversation and debate.

This close to Ruthven, however, he noticed what Ruthven was wearing – deep blue breeches, and a simple white shirt. Nothing else, save for a collar around his throat.

Aubrey scowled. "Why do you wear those collars? Where did you get them?"

He had noticed Ruthven wearing them, but only distantly, far more interested in avoiding him altogether. This was the first time he'd paid real notice since the night Ruthven had become his Pet. That collar had been supple black leather.

This one was deep blue velvet, with a small burst of wisteria stitched on the left side.

Ruthven reached up to touch it. "I like them, master."

"You really do not need to call me that," Aubrey said irritably. "My name is Aubrey – Brey, if you like."

"I like 'master'," Ruthven replied, and leaned forward, until he was close enough Aubrey could smell the tea he was drinking, a hint of flowers and velvet and cologne that smelled of peach blossom and apple. "Unless, of course, my master finds it displeasing that I regard him so."

"Do as you wish," Aubrey said hastily, taking a step back, retreating to his desk.

He thought he heard Ruthven laugh, but dismissed it. "Is there more of that tea?"

"I will ring for it," Ruthven replied, and shoved back the blankets in which he'd wrapped himself.

Aubrey saw he had no shoes, only stockings.

Shaking his head, he pulled out his own book, one he had been reading before all the moving and settling had interfered.

"As to the book, master," Ruthven said, returning to his nest of blankets. It looked cozy, but Aubrey turned from that thought immediately. "I think his reasoning carries serious flaws."

"Oh?" Aubrey said, shutting his book again and leaning back in his seat, crossing his arms across his chest. He'd never argued philosophy with a Pet before; perhaps it would prove interesting.

A couple of hours later, he gave up. "You are remarkably well schooled," he said.

Ruthven shrugged. "I pay attention, master."

"Indeed," Aubrey said. "You are luck you were never caught and killed for being too troublesome to keep."

"Yes, master," Ruthven said, a hint of slyness in his voice.

Aubrey frowned, feeling as though he were missing some joke, hating it. "What other secrets did you keep from your trainers?"

"Only a few," Ruthven said, definitely smirking now. "They are of no interest to you, master." He slid from the window seat and strode to the desk, bracing his hands on it and leaning slightly forward.

The view put his throat, the collar wrapped around it, directly in Aubrey's vision. Ruthven really did have beautiful skin, which the blue velvet only enhanced, though it annoyed him to admit it. "Yes?" he asked, the question coming out snappishly.

Ruthven lowered his long lashes, looking up through them. "It is well past lunch, master."

"Oh," Aubrey said, and saw from the clock on the wall opposite the desk that he was correct. Stifling a sigh, refusing to acknowledge the anxiety that always fluttered in his stomach, he held out his wrist.

It was scarred, now. He really would need to read up on Pets, because he had never really known that they could close up the wounds they opened. It did not completely heal, for there was the scar, but after each...meal...the scar was there.

Aubrey winced as Ruthven bit down, shivering at the odd sensation of his blood being drained away. He wondered if it was a feeling to which he would eventually grow accustomed.

Doubtful, he could not even adjust to the idea that Ruthven would be with him the rest of his life.

No one every stayed long with him; eventually, they all had somewhere else to be. One by one his friends had drifted away, and the knowledge that he would invariably have to return to his family had kept Aubrey from chasing after them, from asking that they stay just a little longer.

He wondered where they all were now, and if they would write. Most of them had traveled abroad, to further studies or simply play another year or two before settling into their own responsibilities. Others had scampered off to the city in pursuit of sport or a wife.

Not that he wanted to go to the city, but travelling...well, it hardly mattered.

He shivered again as Ruthven ceased feeding, attempting to pull away but unable as Ruthven kept firm hold of his wrist. His fingers were warm, a few shades darker than his own, completely unmarked, where Aubrey's always seemed perpetually covered in scratches and paper cuts, and smeared with ink stains.

Ruthven lapped at his wrist, tongue wet and warm, and Aubrey tore his eyes away with a silent curse. What was his problem? Was he really so crass and hypocritical to be so affected? Ruthven was beautiful, there was no denying it. Of course he was beautiful, Gille would never have picked out a Pet who was less than perfect.

At last Ruthven released his wrist, and Aubrey withdrew it, immediately reaching for quill and ink, penning a request to his book merchant in the city, jotting down the sorts of books he would like, along with the month's bill.

Setting it aside to dry, he looked around his study, noting the empty shelves that would soon be filled, assuming the weather did not prevent the arrival of his crates.

"Is that your mother?" Ruthven asked suddenly, gazing to the wall opposite the shelves, the same wall in which was built the window seat.

Aubrey did not need to look at the portrait, but he did anyway. "Yes," he said, smiling sadly, ignoring the cold knot of fear that always coiled in his gut. He could not remember that night, but some part of him always would. He hated it.

The portrait was actually of two women – his mother, Lucy, and her Pet, Wilhemina. His mother was beautiful – dark blonde hair and gray eyes, petite and delicate, but vibrant even in paint. She wore a pale blue gown, to match the pale green worn by Wilhemina, who was a bolder beauty next to his daintier mother. They sat side by side on a stone bench, surrounded by the garden his mother had so loved. Together, the two women held a bouquet of vivid red chrysanthemums.

They looked happy, proud, so very alive.

Once, the portrait had hung in his father's salon. After his mother's death, he had apparently ordered it destroyed. Aubrey had found it buried away in the attic when he was young, while searching desperately for a place to hide from his infuriating cousin.

The portrait was unsigned, something which had always puzzled him, but Aubrey was grateful simply to have it.

"She is beautiful," Ruthven said. "The other woman was your father's Pet, back then?'

"What?" Aubrey said, frowning in confusion. "No, of course not. Mina belonged to my mother. My father did not acquire a Pet until several years after they died. Why did you think Mina belonged to my father?"

"But—" Ruthven stopped, and shook his head. "A mistake. I should know better than to make assumptions. My apologies, master."

Aubrey stared at him a moment, but at last shrugged it off. "I do not believe my father ever had a Pet, before Elisabeth.

But, what little people have told me about him, my father and his brother used to be quite the men about town. He did not settle down until he met my mother."

"I am sorry he lost her then," Ruthven said quietly.

The solemnity of his tone drew Aubrey up short, and he found he was staring again, but Ruthven's eyes were fastened on the portrait.

Finally he just nodded. "I am told he was quite different when she was around. I wish she still were."

Ruthven finally pulled his eyes away from the portrait. "She lives on in her children, in memories, in the way she is still loved and will be always. You look much like your father, but you have her smile and grace."

Aubrey rolled his eyes. "Grace? Perhaps you should consult a dictionary and confirm you know the proper meaning of that word. I assure you, I do not possess grace."

"Yes, master," Ruthven said, but his tone this time was not respectful. Instead, it was as though Ruthven was not trying very hard to hide his amusement. He looked at Aubrey directly, dark eyes holding some deep spark.

It made Aubrey's cheeks hot, that spark, and he jerked his gaze away, eyes falling upon the letter to his book merchant.

Ruthven abruptly snatched it up, and stepped away from the desk.

"Give that back," Aubrey snapped. He stood up and moved around the desk to take it back, furious that Ruthven would just invade his privacy so – even if it was just a list of books he wanted.

He was just reaching out for the letter when Ruthven lowered it and stepped forward, and Aubrey found himself hastily taking a step back – and another, and another, until he collided with the desk, grunting in surprise.

Ruthven set the letter down, hands falling on either side of Aubrey, a playful smile curving his too-pretty mouth. "If you want to know about Pets, master, I am more than happy to answer all your questions."

Aubrey scowled. Ruthven was standing entirely too close, and he did not like the fact his Pet had pinned him so neatly. That feeling prickled along his skin again, the sense that for all he was a Pet, Ruthven was not the submissive type. "What are you?" he demanded. "Are you really a Pet?"

"Of course, master," Ruthven said. He opened his mouth, displaying the unmistakable fangs that marked Pets more clearly than anything.

He still smelled like peach blossom and apple, overlaid with hints of velvet and silk, a touch of sweat and the lingering traces of tea. Aubrey breathed in the tangle of scents, heady and distracting. He tried to glare, but instead found himself captive.

So dark. Ruthven's eyes were so dark, and even when they were a mere breath apart, he could not tell their true color. They looked like night, like the sun had finally set and nothing but shadow remained. Not truly black, but too dark for any one real color to shine through.

They stood that way for a minute or an eternity, he could not tell which. It was only the chiming of his clock, striking the second hour of the afternoon, which finally broke the strange spell. Jerking, Aubrey turned his head away. "Get away from me," he said curtly.

Ruthven promptly pushed off the desk, stepped back, and dipped his head and shoulders in an elegant half bow.

"What in the hell are you?" he asked again.

"Yours," Ruthven replied. "Nothing more or less."

"Ridiculous," Aubrey said. "You drink tea, you read, you act like no Pet I've ever met."

"How would you know, master? With all due respect, you do no like Pets, and avoid them. How, then, do you know the way they behave?"

"You are impertinent," Aubrey replied, moving to sit behind his desk once more, feeling slightly dizzy from the loss of blood, but stubbornly ignoring it.

He did not look up as he heard Ruthven return to the window seat, but continued to sort through the paraphernalia he had unpacked but not sorted and put away.

"Do you really dislike me so, master?" Ruthven asked, some time later.

Aubrey paused in the process of sorting through his book lists. "What?" He frowned at Ruthven, who stared implacably back, face devoid of expression, and from this distance the eyes may as well be pure black.

It was more than a little disconcerting, but Aubrey refused to give in to the foolish emotion. "I neither like nor dislike. I do not know you well enough to make such a decision. I know only that you do not act like any other pet I have ever encountered. Friends of mine, from school, had them. Francois and Elisabeth I have never known to act like you." He shrugged. "I do not care for Pets. It brings me no joy to enslave someone."

Ruthven smiled, then lowered his lashes to look through them in that way that drove Aubrey crazy. "I am your willing slave, master."

"There's no such thing," Aubrey snapped. "No one wants to live such a life."

"If you say so, master."

Aubrey ignored him, and went back to pouring over his lists.

Willing slave. Ridiculous.

They remained that way, Aubrey working, Ruthven silent in the window seat, until Carmilla knocked softly upon the door, and peaked her head in to announce that dinner would be ready in an hour and he should go get freshened up.

Rhododendron

(chapter four)

Stregoni woke with a jerk, disoriented, fumbling automatically for his spectacles even as he heard the noise which had woken him – a frantic banging upon the front door of the apothecary.

Someone was in trouble.

Shoving his spectacles on his nose, he threw back his blankets and slid naked from bed, shivering as he fumbled in the dark for his clothes. He'd just buttoned his breeches and pulled on a shirt when his bedroom door flew open.

His mother was in her sleeping gown, a night robe thrown hastily over it, the belt loosely tied. Her long, curly hair glowed like dark fire in the light of the candle she held. "Stregoni."

"What is it mother?" he asked, taking note of the trembling, shadowy figure behind her. "I'm nearly dressed." He sat down in a nearby chair to pull on his stockings, then fumbled for his sturdiest boots and stamped into them.

"It's Louis, from Blackfield," his mother said, stepping back as Stregoni finally emerged.

Out in the hallway, closer to the light, he could see now it was Louis. A footman for the Blackfield family now, his parents still lived only a few houses down from the apothecary. He was a few years than Stregoni, but they had always got on growing, when their paths crossed.

"What's wrong?" Stregoni asked, stifling a yawn. He had never been very good at waking up, despite the fact both his parents were bright, early risers.

"It's Tony," Louis said, and Stregoni could not tell if he was shaking from fear or cold – probably both. "He's taken a nasty turn, but Lord and Lady Blackfield won't summon anyone. They're too taken with that new 'expert' of hers from the city." His lip curled, despite the trembling.

"What expert?" Stregoni asked sharply, suddenly much more awake. "She mentioned nothing to me about it; she did not even write to cancel my regular visits." A quack, if that curled lip was anything by which to judge.

He bit back a few expletives of his own – this would not be the first time he'd run across a damned quack and his so called miracle cures.

Striding down the hallway, he threw open the door which led to the front half of the building, given over entirely to the apothecary his family had owned and operated for three generations now. Stregoni often felt guilty that there would be no fourth generation.

He could not, in good conscience, attempt to love and lie with a woman when he was so stupidly—

Cutting off the distracting thoughts, he moved quickly to gather all that he would need for an impromptu journey to the Blackfield Estate. Normally, he would not be due to make a trip there until early next week. He had only come a few days ago from his stay with Carmilla.

Thoughts of Carmilla invariably led to thoughts of Gille, and so Stregoni shoved them ruthlessly away once more. He would not be distracted when he was needed.

He frowned as he picked up a tin and discovered it was empty. "Mother, do we have any more camomile?"

"Yes, dear," his mother said in her gentle way. No matter how crazy things might get – and in their occupation, life was seldom anything but – her voice was always calm. Even his father's death, she had taken quietly and calmly, though he suspected she had not been that way once her door was closed.

She rifled through an assortment of cases and tins, then came back with his refilled, kissing his cheek briefly. Turning away, she took up a few more bottles and tins and boxes, tucking them neatly into his bag. "Go quickly, but do not be too reckless. If you can, stay there until the snow clears. It has only gotten worse since we went to bed."

Reaching out, she combed through his hair, mouth pursed in worry. "You did not even fetch a collar," she said, clucking in gentle disapproval, but there was a faint smile in her voice that took any sting from the words. "Go on with you then, and be careful."

"Yes, mother," Stregoni said, and kissed her cheek. "Louis, remain here until the snow clears." He held up a hand to forestall protest. "I can travel faster alone." Without another word, he strode to the entryway, snatched up his cloak, then headed outside and down to the public stable where he kept his horse.

It took only minutes to saddle his horse, though he did it with much yawning and fumbling and shivering.

Finally he led his horse outside, then mounted and took off as quickly as he dared down the street. The snow here, thankfully, had mostly been tamped down or brushed away.

Outside the town, the going was much more difficult. The best Stregoni could do was urge his horse on while burrowing deep into his cloak, pulling a scarf up over most of his face. His spectacles he finally had to tuck away, though he hated not being able to see clearly – but they were so covered in snow, he couldn't see anyway.

Trusting the horse, knowing where and when to guide it, shivering in the biting, bitter cold, he pushed onward.

The going got much easier once they reached the cover of the forest. As they reached a fork in the road, he reluctantly guided the horse to the right, rather than the left.

It was dark, the hour indeterminable, though he suspected it was some wretched hour of the early morning. With the snow and the dark, the screaming quiet brought by both, he felt as though he travelled through a dream.

He wanted nothing more than to take the left path, stumble into the kitchen of the Sangre mansion, find a cup of tea and a good breakfast, maybe find Aubrey or Carmilla to talk for a time.

Instead, he pushed on toward Blackfield, hoping that all he had before him was a simple argument, a quack who would be easily routed.

What was probably only an hour, but felt like a day, later he at last saw the dark stone blur that was Blackfield Manor. The long drive was lined with the blackthorn bushes that gave the manor its name, and more of the same were clustered around the house itself. Come spring, they would burst with green leaves and white flowers, but right now they were nothing but dark, twisting, barren branches.

More falling from his horse than dismounting, he pulled out his spectacles and settled them in place. Hastening into the stable, he was grateful to see a stable hand was awake – likely wakened by Louis, and told to await his arrival. Handing over his horse, he took his bag and strode quickly back to the house, eschewing the front door to slip around take the servant's entrance.

Despite the early hour, the kitchen was bright and warm and bustling. Stregoni left behind the feeling of living in a waking nightmare and slid gratefully back into the world of the waking. He smiled at the cook, and the head footman as he slipped into the room looking more asleep than awake – though he woke up sharp enough as he spied Stregoni. "Doctor!"

"Louis sent me," Stregoni explained. "How is Tony?"

"Not well," the head footman said. "I had wondered where Louis got to, when I did not see him up and doing his morning chores. I was just going to toss him out of bed. Master Tony is asleep from sheer exhaustion. That *doctor,"* he sneered the word, "is killing the poor boy more than saving him."

Stregoni nodded. "May I see him?"

"I will try," the head footman replied. "Lord and Lady Blackfield are determined their new doctor will save the boy, and are not tolerating any protests to the contrary." He motioned, straightening his clothes as he turned to lead Stregoni from the kitchen.

"Come back here when you're done, dear," said the cook with a warm smile. "You look in sore need of a cup of tea."

"That would be lovely," Stregoni said as he departed. They made their way upstairs quickly, spilling of the servant's entrance to the second floor and striding briskly down the hallway to a room near the master room.

He started to open the door when it abruptly swung open from the inside, and he was brought face to face with a man who might have been handsome, save for the oily look about him. His hair had a wet, shiny look to it, short and cut close to his head – literally an oil look there. But there was a gleam to his eye, a cruel set to his mouth, that Stregoni had seen more times than he liked to count.

That expression was always there, in men who made money by banking on the desperation and pain of others. Being a doctor was hard enough, he despised quacks.

"Who are you?" the quack demanded peremptorily. "You don't look like a delivery boy."

Stregoni glared. "I am Stregoni Benefici, the family physician. Who, sir, are you?"

"William," the man said, his fingers going to touch the costly-looking jeweled yellow lily nestled in the over abundance of lace at his throat.

It reminded Stregoni abruptly that he had forgotten his own stock in his haste, and given that haste – he must look quite the mess. What should it matter, though? Ignoring the looks the man was giving him, he shoved the fool hard, then strode past him and deeper into the room.

Tony, only eight years old, was fast asleep. He was nearly buried in piles of blankets, braced against a great many pillow. He was red and sweating, obviously suffering a fever. Stregoni set down his bag and stripped down to his shirt, rolling the sleeves up to keep them well out of his way.

Then he set to work stripping aside blankets, at last finding the small body buried beneath them all, the poor thing soaked with sweat and reeking of some foul concoction. Frowning, he gingerly began to remove the ruined clothes.

"Bring me warm water, a cloth, soap," he ordered, not bothering to look up to see who would do as he said, attention only for Tony. "What in the hell did you give him?" he asked, grimacing at the substance smeared all over Tony's torso.

William appeared like a snake at his side. "A healing ointment, too complex for you to understand."

Stregoni ignored him, and instead brought his fingers to his nose, smelling the substance. "Some of these are toxic!" he bellowed. "If ingested they could cause harm, and I wouldn't be surprised if they give him some sort of rash!"

Rising to his feet, he grabbed William by the lapels of his expensive velvet jacket and shook him hard. "You are a quack and I will see you taken up by the authorities if you do not vacate these premises—"

"Benefici!"

He let go, but only reluctantly, as Lord Blackfield strode into the room, his face a thundercloud.

"My lord—"

"What is the meaning of this?" Blackfield demanded. "I did not ask you to come here. Who sent you? I will see him turned out."

Stregoni ignored the question. "I was informed a quack was taking advantage of you and stood to harm Tony. I came at once – and I see my informant was correct."

"You overstep yourself," Blackfield said coldly. "Doctor William comes highly recommended from a dear friend, and I do not appreciate your tone, nor your implication that I would be so easily taken in by a quack."

"I am the family physician," Stregoni said stubbornly. "I swore to look to the health of this family, and I am doing so, whether you approve my methods or not. Your son is sick, it is not the sort of illness from which he will ever completely recover. My father knew this disease, as did his father. I am ever watchful for new discoveries where it is concerned, but I tell you right now there is none. That substance smeared on his chest is poison, and likely making his fever worse. This man will kill your son."

William stepped forward. "I do not like to presume, but you hardly look like a man whose medical word can be trusted."

"I was more concerned with the health of the child than my own appearance," Stregoni bellowed, shaking with fury and humiliation that these people he had served so long would cast him aside as though he were a useless incompetent. "A doctor who can afford to dress himself in velvet and jewels is more concerned with his money than his patients. If my father were here, he would say the same."

"You overstep yourself," Blackfield said.

"You are a fool," Stregoni replied.

He grunted in pain, reeling back, as Blackfield backhanded him.

His spectacles went flying, but Stregoni did not yet go to retrieve them. "If that is how you feel," Stregoni said, "then I can only say I am sorry for the boy. He does not deserve to suffer like this, because you will not listen to me. I have always served you faithfully and reliably."

"My son is still sick, and he grows worse. Doctor William has done better than you."

Stregoni ignored his throbbing cheek, the blood he could feel dripping from his split bottom lip. "He has not, but you are welcome to think as you like. That man," he hissed, pointing at William, "is a charlatan, and I only hope you see reason before you have cause to regret it."

"I think it would be best if you left," Blackfield said.

"Please," Stregoni said, "allow me to finish tending the boy. He needs to be bathed, given tea and broth."

William's hand fell heavy on his shoulder.

Stregoni's temper snapped, and he shoved hard. "Do not touch me," he said.

William lunged, fist flying.

He went down hard from the punch, not having expected such a level of violence, his entire face throbbing now.

"You have upset this family enough," William. "Leave before I make you."

"Fine," Stregoni said, and retrieved his jacket and cloak, his bag and spectacles, still ignoring his now badly bleeding lip as he stormed from the room.

It was beyond comprehension, though sadly he had seen it before. Still – how many years had he helped this family?

He had done so much, had tended Tony from the very beginning. His mother had attended the birth, and the family's medical history was well documented in one his father's numerous books, as well as his own.

Dismissed like a low, incompetent servant, treated like a mongrel by a velvet-skinned snake.

"Doctor Benefici!" the cook exclaimed. "Oh, my word – I will kill that quack myself, I vow it."

He smiled faintly, wincing as the motion pulled at his lip. It would need dressing before he dared go out in the snow again. "If you are still willing, I would appreciate that cup of tea."

The cook nodded and bustled about the kitchen getting it.

Stregoni set his bag down and rifled through it, coming up with a tincture that he daubed on a bit of cloth brought to him by one of the kitchen maids. Lip cleaned, he dipped the cloth in a bowl of water and quickly washed off the rest of his face.

"How bad does it look?" he asked, striving for levity, as the cook set down a cup of tea and a plate of food.

The cook refused to find it amusing. She scowled in disapproval. "I've half a mind to go up there and show the little weasel what my fists can do, let's see him find a cure for that!" She nudged the plate forward. "Eat that, you'll need your strength. I'm sorry you came out here only to be treated like that, and you always so good to us." Shaking her head, muttering further disapproval, she moved about the kitchen to finish preparing breakfast.

Several minutes later the head footman reappeared, face troubled. "Doctor, you might want to be leaving shortly. His Lordship doesn't trust that you have left, despite repeated assurances."

"I was just on my way out," Stregoni said promptly, finishing the last of his tea before shrugging into his jacket, then swinging his cloak up over his shoulders.

Bidding them all a farewell, he swiftly made his way outside and to the stables, where his horse awaited him. Ignoring further apologies from the stable hand, he mounted and rode off.

Despite the tincture, his lip still throbbed.

He removed his spectacles once more as the snow proved too much for them, tucking them away and closing his eyes, wishing desperately for his bed – wishing more than he was still tending Tony, sick at heart at the idea the boy might die because his parents were fools. Desperate, scared, but fools all the same.

"Home," he muttered, knowing his horse knew the way, praying they would get there swiftly and safely.

Though he tried to stay awake, pain and tiredness combined to get the better of him, and he found himself jerking awake often, the world a blur of gray and white and black all around him, the forest blending into the snow, the dark gray of the morning sky, and Stregoni realized he had no idea how long they had been travelling.

He drifted again, unable to focus for long, and wondered if perhaps the cold was getting to him more than he realized. Some time later, his horse abruptly stopped, nickering in the quiet morning.

They were not in town, Stregoni knew that immediately. By this time, the town would be noisier, and if nothing else he would smell it. Right now, he could smell nothing, though perhaps that was simply that his nose was frozen.

Falling from the horse, he struggled to his feet and brushed snow from his clothes, then fumbled for his spectacles.

He stared as he got them on, and realized where he was.

What in the hells was he doing here?

"Horse!" he snapped. "You don't even know this place! No one knows this place. How did we get here?" He paused to draw a breath, but before he could start issuing threats in earnest, the door behind him opened.

"What in the hell are you doing here, Carrot?"

Gille's voice struck him like a whip, and Stregoni flinched, turning around slowly. "I don't know—" He began, but even as he spoke Gille was plunging down the stairs.

He was grabbed roughly by the shoulders, and shaken hard. "What?" Gille demanded, voice full of fury. "You have no business being here, I demanded to know why you have come!"

Stregoni was getting sick of being mistreated, and he most definitely was not in the mood to struggle with Gille. Even half asleep and in pain, he could not help but notice how wonderful the bastard looked, how fine he smelled.

His eyes stung, his whole body ached with a need to simply be held, to be told everything was all right, or would be – and Gille never would do such a thing, and it was stupid of him even to think about it.

"Unhand me!" Stregoni snapped. "My horse came here, I've no idea why."

Gille narrowed his eyes.

"It's the truth," Stregoni said, yanking down his scarf to be heard more clearly. "I have no desire to—"

"What in the hell!" Gille roared, but before Stregoni could speak, his arm was taken roughly and he was all but dragged up the stairs and into the house, then more or less thrown into a small parlor. "Stay there," Gille hissed. "Do not speak, do not leave this room, do not make so much as a peep – do you understand me?"

Too confused and tired and sore to figure out what was going on, or how to protest, Stregoni simply stood numbly as the door was pulled shut – and locked.

Finding the nearest seat, some worn and faded green thing that had not been cleaned in a long time, Stregoni dropped down into it and fell asleep almost immediately.

He was jerked awake by a familiar touch, and blinked blearily at Gille, whose expression was unreadable.

"Come on," Gille said tersely. "We are returning to Sangre Manor. If you say a single word before we are away, I will throttle you."

"Go ahead," Stregoni said irritably. "It would be an improvement upon the day."

Gille said nothing, though Stregoni caught a derisive snort. He started to make a sharp retort, but simply could not muster the energy.

Instead he went meekly along as Gille dragged him back outside, down into a carriage. It was old, and smelled of dust and disuse, but seemed sound enough. "What—"

"We can hardly ride back, the state you are in, doctor," Gille said, voice flat, as though he were stating some boring fact. Or an annoyance.

Stregoni recoiled from it, hating the lump in his throat, fisting his hands to still their trembling. He was tired, that was all. Tired often led to stupid, and he knew better than to let Gille get to him. "I am sorry to be a burden upon you," he said stiffly, wishing he could sound colder, as uncaring as Gille. "I do not know why my horse took me to your father's house."

"The horse is much like his master, I guess," Gille said.

He flinched again, and did not try to sort out what precisely that meant – that he was stupid, likely.

"Who hit you, Carrot?"

"It is none of your business," Stregoni replied. He closed his eyes and willed himself to ignore Gille, ignore everything, but he was could no more ignore Gille than he could stop breathing.

Through the scent of dust and decay that permeated the carriage, he could smell Gille. His cologne was as sumptuous and fine as always, aspen and Carolina rose, mixing with the heady, musky scent that was all Gille.

He wanted to lean into him, find solace, but finding solace in Gille was like expecting warmth from snow.

Stregoni jerked as a hand grasped his chin, the supple leather of Gille's gloves warm against his skin, though the grip itself was hard enough to bite.

His eyes widened as Gille took his mouth, lip splitting anew as he took no care with the kiss, if the furious and bruising press upon his mouth could be called a kiss. He struggled to get away, but trapped by Gille and the carriage, he was helpless to do anything but go along with it, until Gille at last pulled away just enough he could breathe.

"Who struck you?" Gille demanded.

"Why?" Stregoni demanded. "Going to applaud him?"

"Tell me," Gille hissed.

Stregoni remained silent, reaching up with one shaking hand to wipe the blood from his lip, torn between relief and fury that he could not see Gille clearly in the dark confines of the carriage.

The carriage took that moment to hit a rough patch, tossing him about, until he landed awkwardly half on Gille, half still on the carriage seat.

"You like rough treatment, Carrot?" Gille said, voice cold and mocking. "You certainly seem to be seeking it this morning."

"Yes," Stregoni snapped. "I like pain. I told Blackfield to strike me, and William to punch me, and then sought you out to be mocked and treated like a harlot. Go to the devil!" He reached for the carriage door, more than content to throw himself out of it and walk, but was only yanked back for his effort and pinned in place.

"Blackfield, eh?" Something like cold satisfaction laced Gille's voice.

Stregoni wondered what the hell it mattered, but could not muster the energy or the will to ask, and secretly some part of him did not want to know.

Gille said nothing further, and for all they sat close enough their legs just touched, they may as well be miles apart.

He struggled to hang on to his anger, wishing he was brave enough to lash out, to demand things from Gille he would never get, but pain and exhaustion swiftly beat out the emotions that were simply to tiring to maintain. He was asleep almost before he realized it, head lolling to rest against the nearest hard surface, which smelled of aspen and Carolina roses, and warmer by far than anything he'd encountered since being dragged from bed in the dark of the morning.

Quince

(chapter five)

Aubrey settled back in his bath with a long sigh of contentment.

Let the damnable snow keep falling, he was beyond caring for the time being.

The curtains had been drawn in his sitting room, giving him a grand view of the white-drenched landscape. Even the trees were losing against the relentless snow. It had not stopped for more than an hour or two the past few days, and only a couple of days to partly melt after the last snowfall. Very likely, they would not be able to leave the house for the next week or two at least.

He had forgotten how ruthless winter could be here; the weather at school had been much mellower.

It mattered not, because the fire was roaring, he was soaking in near-boiling water, and then fully intended to ensconce himself in a comfortable chair with a generous allotment of blankets and spend the day reading.

Perhaps he'd go find Carmilla and read with her awhile; they could read a play aloud, as they used to do during the long winters. Yes, she'd enjoy that.

Smiling, he closed his eyes and sank deeper into the steaming water and sighed again. The maid who had arranged his bath had taken the liberty of adding scented oils, but he could not find reason to complain. Purple violet mingled pleasantly with peppermint, both melding with the smell of a crackling fire.

Though, beneath it all, he could still catch a hint of the peach blossom that Ruthven seemed to prefer.

He scowled, refusing to think about the damnably confusing Ruthven while he was trying to relax. The Pet had no business intruding, not when Aubrey was finally enjoying some time to himself. He did not even want to contemplate what his Pet might be about – no doubt revealing that he could do yet something else that was normally forbidden Pets.

Sighing, he slowly dragged his eyes open and stared out the window, frowning at the snow.

Reporting Ruthven would be the proper thing to do. A Pet that free and knowledgeable was a danger; there was no telling what he might be conveying to Elisabeth and Francois.

He could not bring himself to do it, however. Something held him back.

Images of Ruthven dipping his head, looking up through his lashes, anything but submissive, flashed through his mind.

Aubrey sat up with a jerk, swearing softly, the bath water suddenly far too hot.

Damn it, he was going to relax!

Forcing himself to lay back down, he closed his eyes again and refused to think about anything.

Stregoni – there was something to think about. He had arrived with Gille just two days ago, looking rather like he'd come out the loser in a fight. Aubrey wasn't certain which was odder – that Stregoni had been in a fight, or that he'd arrived with Gille.

He also wondered where the devil Gille had been, that he would encounter or meet Stregoni and both of them arrive at seven thirty in the morning.

Neither had been terribly forthcoming with answers; Stregoni had offered only the problem of the quack ensconced in Blackfield, and that his horse had taken a wrong turn in the snow, where he had encountered Gille.

Aubrey sensed there was much missing in the telling, but it was not his preference to press where it was not necessary.

He felt as though he were spending his days drifting. He missed the constant work of school – always class, or a meeting, or papers to write and test preparation to be done. Home again, he felt superfluous. It was obvious that in his absence, Gille had filled the role of son and heir far better than Aubrey ever would.

Well, it didn't matter. Once winter was past, perhaps he would just take off and do as he pleased. Playing the good son had accomplished nothing in the weeks since he'd been home. Beyond being set to handle the household accounts and other such tedious work, he had done nothing.

It should not bother him. It didn't bother him – he was simply unused to being idle. His crates had yet to arrive, no doubt stuck somewhere because of the snow. Unfortunate, for cataloguing them properly with the rest of the household collection would have occupied him most of the rest of the winter.

Perhaps he'd help Carmilla with her book of flowers and herbs. Shrugging to himself, annoyed he could not quite seem to relax, Aubrey reached for soap and cloth. It carried the same scent as the oils, purple violet and peppermint. Good, soft, soap, one thing he had missed at school where his funds had been limited to the pittance his father doled out.

Rinsing off, he quickly washed his hair, and then finally stood up. Water splashed everywhere as he climbed from the tub, soaking the mat laid out, glistening on his skin in the firelight. He stretched with a groan and gave in to an urge to yawn, absently reaching out for his bathing rob – only to come up with empty air where it should have been.

He frowned, but even as he turned, the soft, warm fabric of his robe was draped over his shoulders by hands that lingered.

Aubrey whipped around, fumbling with the robe as it tried to slip – and glared. "What are you doing here?" he demanded. His cheeks heated as he hastily did up the robe. How the hell had he not heard Ruthven come in? How long had he been standing there? "When did you come in?"

"Only a moment ago, master," Ruthven said demurely, but there was a spark of mischief in his eyes in the moment before he lowered them.

He was, as ever, too beautiful for Aubrey's peace of mind. He wore dark brown breeches and a white shirt, but nothing else. Either he did not feel the cold, or simply was not bothered by it. Around his throat was yet another velvet collar. Aubrey had thought by this point he had seen all of them, but this one was new – the same delicate, beeswax color as his hair.

"You—" Aubrey raked back his soaking wet hair, moving closer to the fire to ward off the chill he would begin to feel shortly. "Did you need something?"

Ruthven looked up, though he was still partially inclined in a polite half bow. "Only you, master. I came only to see all your needs were properly tended."

Aubrey jerked his gaze away from the dark eyes, cheeks hot. "I'm fine," he said curtly. "If you want to please me," he coughed as he spoke, "then stop calling me master, and stop being impertinent."

"Alas, master," Ruthven said, and Aubrey knew he was smiling now – smirking, really – but did not turn to confirm it. "That I cannot do, for you are my master, and I enjoy calling you so." The sound of movement made Aubrey twitch, but he did not turn to watch Ruthven approach.

Nor, he told himself, did he shiver when he felt Ruthven's warm breaths against his bare skin, as his voice spoke softly close to Aubrey's ear. "And I like being impertinent."

"I've noticed," Aubrey said. "I cannot believe no one ever...took care of you."

"Some vampires are harder to put down than others," Ruthven said, the words barely audible.

Aubrey jerked away, hand going to his ear, where he swore he had felt the barest touch of lips. "What did you say?"

"I like being impertinent?" Ruthven asked, all innocence.

"Not that," Aubrey snapped.

Ruthven persisted with the innocence. "Some Pets are harder to put down than others?"

Aubrey narrowed his eyes. He started to speak, to demand to know what the hell that word Ruthven had used was, because he was pretty certain he had only seen it once, in an old historical tome.

"I'm feeling a bit famished, master. May I?"

Thrown by the abrupt shift, wishing his damned Pet would at least have the decency to make sense, Aubrey gave an automatic nod and started to hold out his wrist – but instead Ruthven stepped close. Too close.

Aubrey gasped as teeth grazed his neck, then bit down sharp, and he reached out for something to hold, gripping Ruthven's arms tightly, eyes growing strangely heavy as his Pet fed. The initial bite hurt, but it was a hazy and distant pain as he struggled to keep his eyes open.

Then Ruthven's mouth was gone, the feeding over as swiftly as it had begun. His tongue lapped at Aubrey's throat, and he was too startled and lethargic to repress a shiver.

Ruthven didn't withdraw though, simply nuzzled his neck, and Aubrey realized he still clung to his Pet for dear life, but his fingers would not obey his command to let go.

Lips brushed his ear again, the touch so soft but he felt it all the way to his bones.

"You taste sweet, master," Ruthven murmured, making Aubrey shiver again, though he could not say quite why. Not the words themselves...something in Ruthven's voice, his tone.

He forced his eyes open, but doing so forced him to meet Ruthven's gaze, drugged anew on the dark eyes. "What..."

Ruthven smiled, more than a little fang in it, and opened his mouth to reply – but a sharp and sudden knock on the door made them both jerk.

As suddenly as it had fallen over him, the strange lethargy vanished, and Aubrey abruptly felt more like his usual self. Face hot, he swallowed and stumbled back. His legs collided with the tub, and he let out a startled yelp before Ruthven reached out and snatched him back.

The knock came again. Aubrey pushed away from Ruthven and struggled to display a calm he did not feel as he walked toward the door. He opened it.

Carmilla smiled at him. "Thank you for the new book, Brey."

He frowned, noting the small, leather bound book in her hands. "I did not give you a new book. I have several for you, but the weather has kept them from reaching me."

"Oh," Carmilla said, her confused frown matching his own. "I wonder who left it for me, then..." She shrugged and smiled, then leaned up to kiss his cheek. "Well, sorry to bother you. Go back to your bath. You smell nice." With a wave, she turned and made her way slowly down the hallway, deep scarlet gown looking like fresh blood in the weak light of the hallway lamps.

Closing the door, Aubrey turned around to confront Ruthven – who sat calmly in one of the chairs by the fireplace, skimming over the book Aubrey had left there to enjoy after his bath.

"What was all that?" he demanded, hand going to his neck, which throbbed with pain. Not a great deal of pain, but it was there, and he wondered if he'd have a bruise come morning.

Ruthven looked up through his lashes. "I was hungry, master."

"That is not what I mean and you know it!" Aubrey said. "Do not take such liberties with my person."

"I like taking liberties with your person." Ruthven looked up, the dark eyes hitting him full force. "Master."

"Well, don't do it," Aubrey managed, breaking eye contact only with great effort. "Leave me in peace."

"Yes, master," Ruthven replied, the words so soft he barely heard them. He did not move as Ruthven stepped past him, though he felt the slight brush of Ruthven's arm against his like it burned.

He wished he knew who to talk to about Pets. His father and Gille were clearly out – if they knew the way Ruthven behaved, they would get rid of him for certain. As confusing and frustrating as Ruthven was, he did not want to see him killed.

Stregoni, maybe, though he had no experience with Pets. He was smart, though, and level-headed. He'd never seen Stregoni completely lose his head over anything – these past days were the worst he had ever seen him, and Stregoni was simply quieter than usual.

Aubrey nodded to himself, liking the idea, but as he moved to get dressed, the wound at his neck throbbed. He grimaced, and tried to picture telling Stregoni all that had transpired – how, precisely, did one go about explaining he was being...seduced? Toyed with? Attacked? What was Ruthven about?

No, he could not explain to Stregoni that he was being tormented by a Pet who didn't seem to fit that role very well at all. Stregoni knew little or nothing about Pets, and he could not see Stregoni foolishly seduced by anyone. His friend had always been far too bright for such nonsense.

Not that he was going to be foolishly seduced either, Aubrey thought with a scowl as he discarded his robe and began quickly to dress. He was many things, but a hypocrite was not one of them. Most of high society might view Pets as little more than bedroom toys, but he was not one of them.

So why did Ruthven seem intent upon it?

Aubrey touched the mark at his throat, moving to the full length across the room to look at it. Sure enough, he could already see the bruise forming. Odd, Ruthven usually was so careful. His wrists poor faint scars, but that was all. The feedings had never left bruises before. What did it meant that this one had?

Letting his hand fall away, he finished dressing and returned to his sitting room. Ringing for servants to take away the bath, he settled down in his chair and retrieved the book Ruthven had been flipping idly through. The scent of peach blossoms hovered in the air around him, and almost without thinking he again reached up to touch the bruise at his throat.

The servants came and went, leaving him eventually in blissful silence. Behind him the snow continued to fall relentlessly, the crackle and pop of the fire the only sound in the room beyond the occasional whisper of a turning page.

He paused only when the light began to grow too dim for him to comfortably read. Lighting the lamps, he promptly returned to his book, not even bothering to call for food, refusing to do anything that would permit his thoughts to get the better of him for even a moment.

It was the sound of his book thumping to the floor which woke him with a start, and Aubrey blinked groggily around the dark room. The fire was mostly dead, and only the weakest threads of moonlight came through the window, making the snow outside seem to glow.

His candle had long since gone out. What time was it?

Yawning, he hauled himself to his feet and struggled to reach the door. Still more asleep than awake, he banged his shins several times before reaching his goal, groggy and grouchy when he finally yanked the door open.

It was quiet, extremely so. The house had the feel of sleep about it, meaning he had slept for several hours and no one had bothered to seek him out or wake him. Had Ruthven gone to bed? Aubrey started to turn back to his room to see, then scowled at himself and continued on toward the main hall, where he could find a clock.

He paused as he reached the upstairs landing, catching movement further down the west wing hall. His own rooms were in the east wing, well away from his father's rooms.

Wondering who else might be awake, or if it was not as late as it had seemed to him, Aubrey moved down the hallway and started to speak – but the sight of what he saw drew him up short, and he hovered back, watching.

Ruthven stood with Elisabeth just outside the full glow of a hallway lamp, hair like dark honey. Elisabeth shook her head, and murmured something Aubrey could not hear – then she slowly held out her hand, pressing something into Ruthven's.

He smiled at her, and started to pull away, but Elisabeth kept firm grasp. Aubrey stared uncomprehendingly as she raised Ruthven's hand to her lips and kissed the knuckles softly.

Soft, warm laughter filled the hallway as Ruthven finally withdrew, cupping her face in one hand and gently kissing Elisabeth's cheek.

Elisabeth smiled at him, then turned and walked down the hall, vanishing into his father's room.

Ruthven turned toward the door he stood before, and Aubrey realized abruptly that Elisabeth had given him a key.

A key to his mother's room.

He watched as Ruthven unlocked the door, and vanished inside.

Scowling, Aubrey stalked down the hall after him.

He hesitated in front of the door. His mother's room was inviolate – no one went in or out, not even his father. In all his years of memory, Aubrey could not remember this door ever being open. It was one of his father's rules.

Reaching out, he lightly traced the design carved into the wood – a rose in full bloom, nestled between two rosebuds.

He heard a soft rustling from inside, and his hesitancy turned back into anger. Pushing the door open, he stepped inside.

"What in the hell do you think you are doing?" he hissed.

Ruthven paused where he stood over a vanity table. "Good evening, master."

Syringa

(chapter six)

"What are you doing?" Aubrey repeated.

Ruthven stood to his full height. "Nothing harmful, master, I promise. I wanted only to look."

"This is my mother's room," Aubrey snarled, stalking toward him, hands balled into fists, all but vibrating with renewed anger. "I cannot believe—"

A finger was placed over his lips, startling him into silence.

"Have a care, master, unless you want your father to find us here."

"Then I could tell him—" Aubrey cut his own words off, realizing just how not well the conversation would go were he to reveal that he had known all along that Ruthven was problematic.

But that was selfish, and this was his mother's room, damn it.

"No one is allowed in here," he said, but hissed the words quietly.

Ruthven laughed softly, light from the hallway making him a just visible shadow. "Then why is it free of dust and well-cared for, master?"

Aubrey opened his mouth, then closed it with a snap. He had noticed that very thing upon entering – there was no odor and feel of dust in the room. He heard the scratch of a match, the noxious smell of sulfur, then a lamp on the vanity table was light, casting a warm orange glow across their small circle of the room.

It really was clean and well-cared for, at least what he could see of it. As though someone lived here still.

He frowned, reaching out almost without thought to pick up a delicate glass bottle which stirred some foggy portion of his mind. He remembered this bottle...

His mother's perfume, of course, but he had never remembered anything about her before. Not really. Vague impression that were like as not pure whimsy.

But as he pulled the stopper and inhaled the scent, it struck him hard, as only a true memory could. He remembered this scent, it was not merely wishful thinking. As a boy, he had not recognized it. Now, he did. Yellow Acacia. There were traces of other things, but the acacia was the dominant scent.

He set the bottle back down slowly, ignoring the way his hand trembled slightly.

The night of his mother's death was a complete blank. He knew from others that they had gone shopping, that he had bought flowers for his sickly sister...

He sort of remembered his father, but not really. Just another vague image grown foggier still with time.

The sound of movement jerked him from his thoughts, and he looked up to see that Ruthven was helping himself to the contents of a writing table. "Ruthven!" he snarled. "We are leaving!"

Stomping across the room, he reached out to snatch away the book that Ruthven held in one hand – spilling the pages out all over the floor. Heaving a sigh, glaring at Ruthven, he bent to begin picking them up.

Ruthven had lit another lamp, making most of the room visible now. It was striking, but pretty. Not at all what he would have pictured – yet he remembered the way his mother smiled in the portrait in his study, and thought perhaps he should not be surprised after all. It had not been the smile of a delicate woman who simpered in delicate pink and eggshell lace.

The walls were painted a rich cranberry, with accents of cream and pale browns and golds.

On a small table near the window was a crystal vase, filled with dried out dog roses, the withered leaves scattered across the table and on the floor.

He bent to gather more pages, crawling over and stretching out to snag one which had landed by the table with the dead roses, slowly righting himself as his eyes absently skimmed the faded writing.

The words *Pet Rally* caught his eye, and despite himself Aubrey started reading.

It seemed to be a journal entry. Not in diary fashion, but a clear and concise documenting of events. A though his mother had been writing a report.

Without even noticing, he moved to sit in the chair, absently brushing off a few dried petals and leaves, utterly absorbed in the page, and all the others which he still held.

He sat in silence as he finished reading what he could of the few pages he still clutched, setting them down amidst the dead petals when he realized his hands were trembling. "My mother..."

Ruthven's steps were soundless, but Aubrey heard him anyway. Felt him, maybe. He sat on the arm of Aubrey's chair, taking Aubrey's hand in one of his own. "Master?"

"She..." Aubrey shook his head and looked up. "My mother hated the situation with Pets. She hated they were slaves, that they were treated as Pets. She was fighting for their freedom. These journal entries are all about the rallies and fundraisers and meetings she attended. Tons of them, and so much correspondence – she logs what she sent to whom. Quite thorough, she wanted nothing missed."

"Mmm," Ruthven murmured. "That is certainly where you get your thoroughness, then. Your father does not miss things, but he lacks the...focus, I suppose is the word, that you possess. That your mother obviously possessed."

Aubrey looked at him. "You haven't been here long enough to know all that."

"I am observant," Ruthven said mildly. "So you did not know your mother was an activist for the rights of Pets?"

"Of course I didn't know it," Aubrey said. "My father is so strict and old-fashioned, he would never have allowed such behavior in his wife...but she could scarcely keep all this secret." He shook his head. "I had no idea she was so intent upon this."

Ruthven was silent.

"I wonder if it was Mina," Aubrey said. "She must have loved Mina very much."

"Indeed," Ruthven replied. "It is obvious that Mina was as cherished and adored as your mother."

Aubrey nodded. "If my mother loved her that much, of course she was cherished and adored. I'm certain my father loved my mother deeply; he must have indulged her greatly." He let out a soft snort of disbelieving laughter. "I cannot fathom my father being that generous."

"No?" Ruthven asked. "I think you are too harsh."

"Bah," Aubrey said. "I do not think he will ever forgive my defiance is going away to school. My defiance in general. Gille is much more the son he wants." He could not help the bitterness in his voice, though he hated that was saying such things to Ruthven. Something about the setting, the discovery, drew it from him.

Ruthven let go of his hand, then cupped his chin, turning his face and tilting it up. "You do not see as clearly as you should, master," he said quietly. "That seems to be a problem around here. Some of it is willful, some of it is not. The eyes should open to some things...but should remain closed to others. You should speak with your father, I think you are not the disappointment you think, master."

"Stop calling me that," Aubrey said, jerking away. "We both know I am no master to you, for whatever you are, it is no Pet. No Pet in the ordinary sense, anyway. That word you used before..."

"What word, master?" Ruthven asked.

Aubrey reached out to pick up a dried rose petal, rubbing it between his fingers. "Vampire," he said softly. "That's what you said before – vampire. That word has not been used for more than a century."

"I must have read it somewhere," Ruthven said with a shrug.

"You're a liar," Aubrey said. "I simply cannot tell if you're a poor one, or far too good a one."

Ruthven grinned, all fang. "Which would you prefer I be, master?"

"Honesty," Aubrey snapped. "A normal Pet."

"What is a normal Pet?" Ruthven asked, and Aubrey realized his chin was still held fast by Ruthven's fingers. "Elisabeth? Francois? Mina?"

Aubrey scowled, and retorted, "Not you."

Ruthven laughed, and let him go, fingers pulling away slowly in a lingering caress.

Pretending he did not feel a lingering touch upon his face, traces of warmth, Aubrey gathered up the papers and stalked to the writing desk. Sitting down, he began slowly to sort them as best he could, lingering over the pages he had not read, losing himself once more to the words written by the woman who had been his mother, who had been brutally murdered by bandits more than a decade ago.

"What were you doing in here, Ruthven?" he asked a few minutes later, as he carefully set the journal back on the writing desk, then pulled the cover down over it before sliding the chair back into place and stepping away.

He wanted to stay, to read more, to learn more – his mother had had hated the slavery as much as he did...but she had done something about it. What had Aubrey ever done, but complain and avoid Pets as much as possible?

She had harassed and cajoled and fought and argued and made a stand. He'd done none of that. If she had lived, would he have wound up helping her? Would she be disappointed in him now?

He rather thought she would. His fingers twitched, and Aubrey barely resisted an urge to open the writing desk once more, to glean from it all he could about his mother, about Mina, about the cause his mother had fought on Mina's behalf.

"You look as though heavy thoughts weight you down, master," Ruthven said, his calm voice almost soothing.

It just annoyed Aubrey further.

"I was thinking about my mother," Aubrey replied. "I wonder if she would still be doing this, now. If she would have accomplished something by now...if I would be helping her."

Ruthven quirked one thin brow. "Master?"

Aubrey frowned in thought. "Do people still try to free the Pets?"

When he replied, Ruthven's voice was so soft Aubrey could barely hear him. "There will always be a voice of dissent, master."

Nodding, decided, Aubrey spun away from the desk. "I am going to continue what my mother began."

"What?" Ruthven asked, and for once that cool voice slipped, surprise slipping into it. "Master, I do not—"

Aubrey spun around to face – and collided hard, breath whooshing out of him. He stumbled back, but was caught about the waist by Ruthven. He blinked up at Ruthven, the words he'd been about to say skittering away, forgotten.

Ruthven stared back, eyes unfathomable in the weak light, a tall shadow with the lamps behind him.

"What were you doing in here, Ruthven? Do not think I've forgotten you have not answered me that question."

"Only looking, master," Ruthven replied.

Aubrey snarled. "Stop calling me that! We both know you use it mockingly."

Ruthven shook his head. "No." He leaned in close, until his words were almost more an impression than actual sound, so close that Aubrey had only to twitch and those lips would be against his, and he hated himself for even thinking it. "Your blood I have tasted, and so to you I belong."

He shifted, and Aubrey jerked, shoving hard, the movement causing him to stumble, taking the hard fall on his backside from which Ruthven had saved him a moment ago.

Grunting in pain, he slowly dragged himself back to his feet.

Ignoring Ruthven, deciding he would get answers later, he started to stalk back to his own room.

Ruthven's words drew him up short. "Is this really what you want to do, master? Attempt to free Pets?"

"Yes," Aubrey said. "It's what my mother would want."

"That is what you want? For me to be free?"

Aubrey turned around. "You don't want to be free?"

"It's not about whether I want freedom," Ruthven replied, walking toward him, hair gold again in the light of the hallway lamps, skin gleaming where it was not covered by dark silk. "I asked if you want me to be free?"

He stared at Ruthven long and hard. "You're a Pet. You should not be a slave, even if you are the most confounding Pet I've ever encountered or heard about."

"You think me so unusual? Yet you know nothing about Pets, you have said so yourself."

Aubrey shrugged. "Then the first step is the one I have already begun – learn more. I do not particularly care, though. Slavery is slavery, and no man should be a slave. Being under my father's thumb brings me no joy. Anyway, my mother devoted her life to the cause. That must mean something. I'm tired of discussing this. We are going back to my room, and you are giving me the key to my mother's room."

"I cannot," Ruthven said. "I promised to return it."

Aubrey scowled, but nodded "To Elisabeth."

Ruthven was silent a moment. "Yes, master."

Which reminded him of the bizarre exchange between them. "Why did she kiss your hand?"

"I do not know, master," Ruthven replied, and as quickly as that he was his false, demure self again, bowing low, looking at Aubrey through his lashes. "Maybe she simply thought I was that pretty."

Aubrey snorted. "Pretty is as pretty does. If you appear as what you are, Ruthven, then I would say you look like trouble."

Ruthven grinned, and bent in a deep, formal bow. "You flatter me, master."

Rolling his eyes, refusing to be amused by the situation because there was nothing funny about any of this, Aubrey turned away and resumed his walk down the hall. He paused as he reached the main landing, realizing for the first time that he was hungry.

"I'm going to get something to eat," he said as Ruthven drew up close.

"Yes, master," Ruthven replied, and his tongue flicked out briefly to lick his lower lip. Slowly, the barest hint of fang visible for a moment.

Aubrey turned hastily away. "You can join me or not, as you like – but don't touch me. You fed earlier, and I know you had more than enough."

"I can never have enough of you, master."

"Ruthven!" Aubrey hissed, drawing to an abrupt halt on the stairs, turning sharply around to glare. "Cease that nonsense at once!"

Mouth quirked in a smile that held entirely too much smirk for Aubrey's taste, Ruthven leaned down until their noses were just barely touching. "No. Master."

With that, Ruthven moved past him, strolling down the stairs as casual as could be.

Aubrey was left sputtering. "You! You are incorrigible, and sorely in need of a thrashing."

Ruthven stopped at the foot of the stairs, grinning up at him. "I did not know you liked such things, master."

His face suddenly felt as though it might burst into flame. "Ruthven!" he hissed, unable to believe what he was hearing.

"Yes, master?" Ruthven asked, all innocence.

Aubrey quickly finished descending the steps. "You—" His reprimand faltered as he caught the faintest hints of music. Piano. Someone was in the music room at this horrendous hour? "Who the devil is in the music room?"

"I could not say, master," Ruthven replied. "Did you want to beat him too?"

"You!" Aubrey sputtered. "Do not say such things. I do not permit it."

Ruthven dipped his head. Aubrey wanted to tear his eyelashes off, that look drove him positively mad – and he rather suspected Ruthven knew it. Infuriating Pet. "Shall we adjourn to the kitchen, master?"

"You did not agree to stop saying such things," Aubrey said.

"Yes, master," Ruthven said, then turned and walked away, before Aubrey could figure out whether he was agreeing to stop, or agreeing that he had not agreed to stop.

Rubbing at his temples, willing away the headache he could feel forming, Aubrey gave up for the time being and followed Ruthven to the kitchen.

When he reached it, Ruthven was at the farthest end, staring out the wide window over the bank of sinks. Aubrey frowned, for there was something to the set of his shoulders...

"Is something wrong?"

"No, master," Ruthven said absently. "I thought I saw..." He drifted off, and then suddenly leaned forward, one hand braced on the windowsill.

"What is it?" Aubrey snapped, striding across to join him.

Ruthven turned, and caught him by the shoulders. "Nothing, master," he said firmly. "You look sleepy. Sit down and rest a bit, and I will return in a moment."

Aubrey blinked, caught by the dark eyes – and a sudden, overwhelming yawn. "Did you see..."

"Go rest, master. Perhaps you should go to bed, at that, and I will bring up tea and breakfast for you, in a little bit."

He started to argue, but the words only came out a yawn, and before he even realized it Aubrey was leaving the kitchen and returning to the upstairs. Back in his room, he paused long enough only to strip out of his clothes before he climbed into bed and fell promptly to sleep.

Enchanter' s Nightshade

(chapter seven)

Stregoni shivered in the dark cold of the early morning. It was an hour he was truly beginning to hate, and out of doors was not a way to attempt to enjoy it.

His only other option, however, was to return inside.

He would rather freeze to death than listen to the haunting melodies played by a man who only used and discarded him. A man whose hot kisses always made him forget that they hid a stone heart.

The cold numbed, and he needed it. He ached inside and out, body thoroughly and almost savagely used, heart shredded all over again. Would he ever learn?

No, and he knew it, so he may as well stop asking himself that same damn question every time he gave in to the need to let Gille use him.

Why did Gille use him?

Probably, he just liked knowing he had that sort of power. Power was as natural to Gille as breathing.

Stregoni jumped at the sound of another's feet in the snow, spinning around – and drew up short.

"What are you doing out here?" he asked, trying for curt but not quite managing, still raw and shaken from his tempestuous interlude with Gille.

Francois shrugged. "I could not sleep. I wanted a walk. I do beg your pardon, Dr. Benefici."

Stregoni frowned. "Did you get Gille's approval?"

"I did not wish to disturb him," Francois said, then a cold smirk slid over his pretty mouth as he dragged his gaze slowly up and down Stregoni's body. "He seemed busy."

"Watch your tongue and manners," Stregoni said, the words lashing out.

Shame washed through him, but so did jealousy, white hot and bright.

Francois was beautiful. His hair was true black, fine and cut short to frame his almost pretty features. Though the moonlight was not enough to see them clearly, Stregoni knew his eyes were a breathtaking purple, richer than the finest dyes. Like Gille, he was tall and slender. Only Ruthven, Stregoni thought, could rival Francois in the beauty department.

Next to him, Stregoni felt truly ugly. He could not fathom why Gille touched him at all, except for the thrill it gave him to see Stregoni so low and desperate.

He didn't hate Francois for his looks, though. No, he hated Francois because for all he was a Pet, he was close to Gille. He shared Gille's bed, was treated with accord, went with him about the city and town, conversed with him a friendly manner...

Francois knew Gille in a way Stregoni never would, had Gille in a way Stregoni would never know.

"Get back inside," he said curtly. "Do not wander about without your master." Not waiting for a reply, he turned and stalked away, moving closer to the dormant and frozen weeping willow opposite the small frozen pond that occupied this side of the house.

He stared at the pond, wondering how thick the ice was, how cold the water – cold enough he would feel it, or would it numb him instantly?

For one fleeting moment, he was tempted to find out. He'd taken a step forward, boots crunching in the snow, when a sudden wash of lethargy struck him. He yawned, nearly dropping to his knees, and slowly stepped back, well away from the pond.

The back of his knees collided with a bench, and he more fell than sat down upon it, heedless of the snow which could not penetrate the solid cloak which had been a gift from Carmilla last winter.

He looked up as Francois approached. "Get back inside. I cannot think the consequences for your disobedience are worth a jaunt in the snow."

"Oh, I think the chance to speak with you, doctor, will make my punishment well worth it," Francois, voice smooth as silk, and as slick as the ice covering the pond.

Stregoni felt a chill that had nothing to do with the cold. "Why would you want to speak with me?"

Francois smiled in a way that flashed his fangs.

He repressed a shiver, and stood up, refusing to appear as though he were cowering before what was in reality little more than a piece of property.

"I wanted to know," Francois said, still baring his fangs, "what he finds so interesting in an ugly little thing like you.

Stregoni flushed with shame and anger. "You are out of line, Pet. Get out of my sight."

"No," Francois said, and strode closer.

The look in his eye sent a pulse of alarm through Stregoni – but it also put his back up. Damn it, he did not deserve this. As Francois approached, he took a step forward of his own and shoved Francois back, looking on in satisfaction as he fell to the snow, clearly taken by surprise. "Get back to your master," he snapped. "Leave me in peace."

Instead Francois lashed out, and with a startled cry Stregoni stumbled sideways into the snow, managing to land so his face was buried in it.

Then he was yanked up, blinking snow from his eyes as he stared up at Francois, whose purple eyes were bright with rage – and something else, which Stregoni almost recognized, before they were abruptly caught in an awkward, angry grappling, and he wondered for a moment why there were acting in such childish fashion.

As he collided roughly with the bench though, hard enough he would likely find a bruise in the morning, Stregoni ceased to care.

"You should be in bed, Pet," he snarled, throwing Francois off and regaining his feet.

"At least I was paid for," Francois snarled. "You seem to give yourself away for free."

Stregoni turned red, and threw a punch before he had time to think, putting every last bit of his misery and pain, shame and humiliation, anger and confusion and frustration, into it.

Francois reeled back – but didn't fall. His eyes almost seemed to glow now, there was so much anger in them.

"It's no business of yours," Stregoni snarled, tensed for whatever Francois did next, "if your Master feels compelled to seek his pleasures elsewhere."

"No, I suppose not," Francois said, abruptly recovering some of his cool composure, though his eyes were still hot.

"Because he always comes back to me after he's done tossing you, doesn't he?"

Stregoni barely resisted an urge to attack him again, and only because he was suddenly struck with realization. He knew what he'd seen in Francois' eyes a moment ago – jealousy. Francois was jealous of him.

"Why?" he asked. "Why are you jealous of me? Why would you do this? You'll be lucky if Gille doesn't beat you should he find this out."

Hate filled Francois' face. "I'm not jealous of an ugly little doctor," he hissed. "I—" His words cut off abruptly, dismay flickering across his face for a moment before his reserved mask fell into place.

Stregoni spun around just as a hand wrapped around his arm, and he was jerked roughly forward.

"What is going on here?" Gille demanded, voice level but full of promise that bad things would happen if a suitable explanation was not provided. He was still only partially dressed, having done nothing more than pulled on his boots and thrown on a cloak before coming outside.

His hair was loose, even, tumbling about his face in a disheveled mess, eyes bright and sharp behind the loose strands

Stregoni ignored the question. "What are you doing out here?" he asked.

Gille shook him hard. "I am asking the questions here, Carrot. Why are you both out here and why does it look as though you have been fighting?" He abruptly let go of Stregoni to stalk to Francois.

"Pet," he said in a silky, menacing tone. "I did not give you permission to leave the house."

"No, master," Francois said, tone quiet, almost mellow. It was clear he knew he was in trouble, but he did not look away from the fury in Gille's face, but met his gaze dead on.

That was when Stregoni saw it, though the flicker of emotion was gone nearly as quickly as it had come.

Francois was in love with Gille – really, truly, as hopelessly in love as Stregoni.

Damn it.

"We were doing fine until you showed up," he said, snapping the words, knowing Gille would hate the tone. "Do me a favor and go away again."

Gille immediately whipped around, eyes snapping to his. He let go of Francois and stalked back to Stregoni. "What is going on..." He blinked suddenly, swayed, and held a hand to his head.

"Are you—" Stregoni stopped abruptly as he was overtaken by a wave of exhaustion and dizziness, and he saw that Francois seemed to be suffering the same.

What was wrong with them?

Then Gille shook himself. "Get inside," he snapped at both of them. "Honestly, walking about in the cold – your both idiots, and the last thing I need is to be burdened with a couple of corpses in the winter. Inside, now, or I'll throw you in the pond myself.

He grabbed Stregoni's arm and dragged him along, turning his head to snap, "Francois! Now!"

Stregoni jerked his arm away. "Do not touch me," he hissed.

"You didn't mind an hour ago," Gille replied, anger fading, replaced by the more familiar cold mockery. "Why were you and my Pet walking about together at this hour?"

Francois walked just behind them, and Stregoni turned to look at him.

He felt a moment of dizzy confusion as he looked at Francois' beautiful face. He'd been utterly certain he would see a split lip, but now he could not think why he had expected such a thing.

They had been walking. Arguing about...or perhaps over...Gille. He'd told Francois many a time to go back inside.

And he remembered figuring out that Francois was as in love with Gille as he – but he could not remember much of it clearly.

"We were discussing how utterly despicable you are," Stregoni finally retorted. "He's too nice to say so, of course, but I am not."

He did not wait for a reply as they returned inside, but threw off his wet cloak and immediately took to the stairs, all but bolting for his room once he reached the second landing.

Stripping out of his wet clothes, he bundled into his night robe and slumped into a chair by the fire that only required a moments work to bring fully back to life.

What had happened?

The whole night was a blur of images and impressions – Gille's hair shining in candlelight, sweat gleaming on his skin as he took Stregoni hard and fast and brutal, the smell of wine, the cold, sharp, scent of winter, the bite of the air.

Angry words, the shocking realization that Francois was jealous of him.

A hazy image of punching someone, of grappling in the snow, but it seemed more like a fading dream than a reality. Had he fallen asleep briefly? Was he so cold and tired that he was confusing tonight's chance meeting with Francois with his fight with William?

He yawned and shoved the thoughts away to deal with come morning.

Standing up, he stumbled his way to bed and tossed his robe aside before burrowing beneath the blankets, asleep before he hit the pillow.

The sound of someone pounding on his door jerked him awake.

"Come in," he croaked, then cleared his throat and tried again.

He'd barely gotten the words out when the door was thrown open and a frantic-looking Aubrey stumbled in. He was barely dressed, hair a tangled mess, eyes wide with fear "Stregoni – it's Ruthven."

"Ruthven?" Stregoni echoed, struggling to wake up. "What's wrong?" He threw back the covers and retrieved his robe from the floor.

If was bothered by the lack of modesty, Aubrey gave no show of it. "He won't wake up. It's like he's dead, but he's still breathing. I don't now what's wrong—he didn't—he went—"

Alarmed by the panic overtaking his normally calm friend, Stregoni grabbed his shoulders and shook Aubrey hard. "Brey! Calm down. Take me to him." Not bothering to take the time to dress, Stregoni made certain his robe was well-fastened, then snatched up his medic bag and all but dragged his friend from the room, doing the leading himself as they made their way to Aubrey's room.

In Aubrey's bed, Ruthven looked fast asleep. He was stretched out on his back, head braced on a pillow, lying under a mount of blankets. He could see where Aubrey had frantically thrown them back in his haste.

Setting his bag down on the bed, Stregoni frowned thoughtfully as he began to examine Ruthven.

First he tried simply to wake him – gently at first, then more firmly with a hard slap to his face.

Nothing.

"Hmm," he murmured, then went systematically about checking his pulse, his breathing, for any sign of injury. "Did you do anything unusual last night?"

Aubrey was silent a moment. "We were up late, exploring the house a bit. We couldn't sleep. Then we went down to the kitchen to get some food and..." He fell silent.

Stregoni turned to see why.

"I don't remember," Aubrey said. "I...we went for food...then I woke up in bed. I don't remember anything else." He placed his fingers to his temples. "Ruthven...Ruthven said something, or saw something. I don't remember! I can't even tell you what we had to eat."

He moved to the bed himself, reaching out to lightly touch Ruthven's cheek. "I was mad at him most of the night, I remember that much," he said quietly.

"Brey, this isn't your fault," Stregoni said, sliding fully into doctor mode. He hadn't thought Aubrey spared a moment's thought for the Pet which had been forced upon him, but he was exhibiting the guilt loved ones always displayed for the family or lover or friend who was ill. "You'll have to tell me in more detail everything you did last night. You said exploring? Where? What did you do? Touch?"

Aubrey was silent, staring hard at Ruthven, obviously lost in thought.

Stregoni grasped his shoulder. "Brey."

"We—" Aubrey finally dragged his eyes away from the sleeping Ruthven. "You can't tell anyone, Stregoni."

"Of course not," Stregoni said, baffled and a little stung, words coming out a bit sharper than he intended. "I'm your friend, and a doctor knows how to be discreet better than anyone."

Aubrey flinched. "I know, I'm sorry. We—I caught him breaking into my mother's room. He never would say why he did it. We poked around..." He looked guiltily away. "Looked through her things. I had no idea—" He drew a sharp breath and shook his head. "Anyway, we touched papers, that was all. Well, and I looked at a bottle of perfume. Then we left, went down to the kitchen. After that, I don't remember anything." He frowned in though. "I went to bed alone, I think. Ruthven must have come in a few minutes later."

He turned back to Ruthven, and for the first time Stregoni noticed the lurid bruise on Aubrey's throat. He reached out reflexively to touch it, pulling back when Aubrey jerked. "What happened, Brey?"

Aubrey turned a bright red, his own hand going up to touch the bruise. "Feeding," he said tersely. "Ruthven fed deep, or got carried away, or something."

Stregoni quirked a brow, wondering what wasn't being said that'd cause his friend to turn that particular shade, but did not press it. "Well, I guess that answers the question of whether or not you've been feeding him thoroughly."

"I wouldn't starve my Pet to death," Aubrey snapped, glaring at him – then he turned away, voice calmer when he spoke again. "Sorry."

Shrugging it off, Stregoni returned to examining his patient, but finally drew back with a shake of his head. "I think he's just sleeping, Brey. There's nothing wrong with him. Heart, breathing, everything seems normal. It's like he's just gone into a deep sleep. He smiled reassuringly. "We'll give him a day or so, then see how he fairs. I know it's hard, Brey, but I don't think you have anything to worry about. It's peculiar, for certain, but I don't see anything actually wrong with him. No fever, he's not too hot or cold, heart beat is true, breathing seems normal, he's healthy looking – just asleep."

Aubrey nodded, obviously wanting to argue but holding back.

"Keep an eye on him, and I'll linger a few days more. Not in a hurry to fight my way through this snow, anyway." He stepped closed enough to embrace Aubrey briefly. "Do not worry upon it, insofar as that's possible."

He only received another nod in reply, but Aubrey also relaxed the slightest bit. "Thank you, Stregoni."

"It's what I'm for," Stregoni replied, and retrieved his bag before leaving them alone.

There was many a question he would like to ask, but his curiosity would have to be appeased later.

He wandered slowly back to his room, lost in thought – and collided with someone else, turning the corner. Shaking his head, he stepped back, offering apologies automatically.

When he looked up, he was staring into the dark purple eyes of Francois, who glared back but said nothing.

Confusion rose up, as he suddenly recalled all that had happened the previous night – and realized that he could remember very little of it. "Did we....talk....last night?" He asked.

"Yes, Doctor Benefici," Francois said, polite but cool – but Stregoni could see that Francois was just as confused.

He opened his mouth to say something, but then closed again, not certain what to say. The only thing from their time outside that he recalled with perfect clarity was that single moment when he realized that he and Francois had one terrible, agonizing thing in common.

They both loved Gille, despite all the reasons not.

Jealousy still crackled between them, but Stregoni could not summon it with the energy he had before. It was hard to hate someone who knew all too well what his particular brand of misery was like.

He bit off an urge to speak, to ask, to sympathize – to do any number of things that would only be stupid.

Muttering another apology, he broke their locked gaze and strode past Francois, back to his own room.

Purple Lilac

(chapter eight)

Aubrey was going insane.

Two days.

For two long, miserable days Ruthven had not stirred. Further examination from Stregoni only gained a reiteration that Ruthven was merely asleep.

Why?

He had torn apart the library looking for something, anything, that would tell him about Pets and illnesses. Illnesses in general. He had even borrowed Stregoni's hoard of medical texts and harassed his friend to death seeking for any sort of clue.

It made no sense. Ruthven had been perfectly fine on their way to the kitchen. What had caused this to happen?

Aubrey held a hand to the fading bruise on his throat. Was it his fault? Had something been wrong with his blood?

Stregoni has warned him he would make himself sick if he kept fretting so, but all he knew was that this must somehow be his fault – why else would Ruthven be like this?

He worried his lower lip as he stared out at the depressing landscape beyond his window.

What did he really know, though? Ruthven, he felt plenty confident in saying, was wholly unique. He didn't know what Ruthven was – except that was most definitely not a Pet.

Turning away from the window, he let his gaze fall once more upon the figure lying far too still in his bed. He'd barely slept himself the past two days, unable to bear using the bed while Ruthven sleep, but not getting much rest by sleeping on his sofa – and he did not want to be far away in a guest room on the chance something happened.

He reached out to touch Ruthven's cheek, willing the damned fool to stir, but he may as well be dead for all the signs of life he displayed. Other than his soft breaths, the warmth of his skin, he could be a corpse.

Aubrey snatched his hand away, snarling a muted curse, wishing Ruthven would wake up already so he could stop worrying himself sick – so he could figure out why this had happened.

Why was there not a single damned book about Pets anywhere in the house? Surely, given what his mother had done, there must be—

His mother's room. Of course. He had been so guilt stricken at the thought of their explorations there being a possible reason for whatever afflicted Ruthven, he had failed to consider the cure might be there as well.

Not giving himself a chance to make excuses, he bolted through the halls – and came to a halt as he realized that he did not have a way inside. The key would be somewhere in his father's room...

His father's room. There would also be a door connecting the two master suites.

Heart hammering in his chest, wishing he knew why he was going to this much trouble for a Pet whom he did not even really like – and who was insubordinate and too intelligent and dangerous – he crept further down the hall to his father's room.

The doorknob twisted easily beneath his hand, and he pushed it slowly open, ducking his head in to verify that his father and Elisabeth were both still downstairs.

It was strange, being here. He'd never been in his father's rooms, not that he could recall, though he probably had been in them as a child.

They smelled like the petunia-scented perfume Elisabeth favored, but he also caught traces of his father's cologne, aloe and cedar leaf. The room was, of course, deeply masculine, but he saw splashes of soft color here and there that indicated his father did not live alone.

Unwilling to look longer, feeling like an invader, Aubrey stepped further into the room. Calling himself suicidal, he dashed across the room as quickly as he could and tried the handle on the door he thought led to his mother's room.

When it twisted easily, he let out the breath he hadn't known he'd been holding.

Closing it behind him, he lingered a moment wit his back against the door, struggling to regain control of his beating heart, his unsteady breaths.

In daylight, the room seemed so ordinary. Clean and bright, it almost looked as though someone still lived here. He felt a pang in his chest, an old one, the lingering wish that his mother was still alive, for surely everything would be better.

Pushing aside the useless, wishful thought, he finally ventured into the room and began to look around for books, or anything else which might prove useful. The writing desk was the most obvious place to begin, and he nearly crowed with excitement and relief as he immediately came upon a book detailing the nature and care of Pets – as well as *A History of the Vampire*.

He drew a sharp breath, unable to believe what he was seeing. Surely a book like this...precious few books were available on Pets, for fear Pets themselves would somehow learn of the knowledge contained within.

No doubt the other reason was people like his mother, who thought Pets deserved to be free and equal citizens. He picked up the book and tucked it with the other one in the crook of his arm, then quickly rifled through the desk for anything else. He was sorely tempted to take away those things he recognized now as being written by his mother, but it seemed wrong somehow. The books he could justify...the personal items, he could not.

A quick perusal of the room revealed nothing else as promising as the books in his arms, though he did grab two more general volumes about Pets.

Finished, he turned back to the door and reached out to grab the knob – right as the door was pushed open, hitting him square in the forehead.

Aubrey tumbled to the ground with a startled cry, freezing as he realized the boots before him were the very last he wanted to see.

Slowly he dragged his gaze up to meet his father's furious expression.

"What in the hell are you doing here?" Sangre demanded coldly, voice just low enough not to be a shout.

"I want to help Ruthven," Aubrey said, rubbing his sore head as he snatched up his dropped books with the other hand, slowly standing up.

Sangre grabbed him by the front of his shirt and all but dragged him out and threw him into Sangre's own room. "You are not permitted here. How the hell did you even know such books might be here to find?"

Aubrey wanted badly to take a step back; he had never seen his father so angry – even defying him to go to school had not resulted in this loss of temper. He refused to play the coward. "I could not sleep three nights ago – I explored. On a whim, realizing I knew nothing about my mother, and decided to learn what I could."

"You did not have my permission to do that," Sangre said angrily. "I have forbidden any of you from entering your mother's room."

"Why?" Aubrey demanded, barely restraining an urge to throw the books at his father. "You didn't want us to know mother fought for the freedom of Pets? That she cared passionately for Mina? Why would you keep that from us? Were you ashamed of her goals?"

He cried out in pain as Sangre backhanded him.

"Do not *ever* suggest that I was ashamed of your mother," Sangre said, so furious he was shaking. "Do not dare."

"Then why did you never tell us?" Aubrey asked, holding a hand to his sore cheek, shaking now himself.

Sangre glared at him. "That is none of your business. If I find any sign that you have been in her rooms again, I will thrash you within in an inch of your life."

"Naturally," Aubrey said bitterly. "If I resumed the work she never finished, I wonder what you'd do – kill me?"

"You will do no such thing!" Sangre bellowed, and Aubrey jumped with the force of it, stumbling several steps back.

He realized with a shock that it wasn't rage making his father tremble – it was fear.

His father was terrified of something.

"Why not?" he demanded. "She was passionate about it – she wanted Mina to be free."

"Yes," his father said, abruptly looking old and weary and sad. "She did. The day we met, she was fighting for that very thing...and she was getting ready for yet another fight when those who opposed her views held up her carriage and murdered them both."

Aubrey dropped the books in shock. "W-what?"

"Fear is a powerful motivator, Brey," his father said, and the pain and fear were obvious, now that Aubrey knew to look for them. "Many people feared – still fear – what might happen to humanity should the blood drinkers gain true freedom. They feared it enough they killed a woman who might very well have proven successful at freeing them."

"Why...why did you never explain this to us?"

"To keep foolish ideas from entering your head," Sangre snapped. "Because there was no need for you to know. She's dead, Mina is dead—" He broke off abruptly, and took a deep, slow breath. "Get out, and I do not ever again want to hear you carrying on about saving Pets. I will beat you within an inch of your life before I permit that."

Aubrey bent to gather up his books. "I'm an adult," he said slowly, stubbornly meeting his father's eyes. "I can make my own decisions, and if I want to follow in my mother's footsteps, that is my choice."

"Not while you are under my house," Sangre snarled. "I forbid it, and that is the end of the matter."

He started to snarl right back that he was more than happy to leave his father's house, but bit the words back at the last, holding the books tight and turning to stomp from the room and back to his own.

Inside, he barely made it to the bed before giving in to the trembling which overtook him. Sick. He was going to be sick.

His mother and Mina had been killed by bandits. Robbers. Bastard thieves who had preyed upon two defenseless women and a child. That's what he'd been told his entire life – yet now, the lie seemed so pathetically obvious.

The stretch of road was a private one. It had never been used, except by his family. It led straight from their home to the town. No other major roads intersected it; only small footpaths that led to the smaller homes of peasants. Robbers would not pick so remote a location; they would choose the more populated highways.

She and Mina had died fighting for the freedom of Pets – and his father had simply buried it? Ordered it forgotten? Hidden it from his children? Damn it, Aubrey had been there! He could have died to, and his father preferred to forget it all?

Why?

He buried his face in his hands, willing his body to stop shaking. Still, he had not expected to hear all that he had learned.

How could his father simply let the matter drop? It made Aubrey want to push, to defy the bastards who had killed his mother and Mina in cold blood.

Yes, that was precisely what he would do, and damn his father or anyone else who wanted to stop him.

First, however, he must save Ruthven. If he could not save one Pet from a strange disease, how could he save all of them from enslavement?

Taking a deep breath, he looked over his books, sorely tempted to go straight to the history – but the more recent treatise on Pets would probably prove to be more useful.

He was astonished he had the books at all. As angry as his father had been, Aubrey had expected him to take the books away, to forbid him to keep them. Yet he hadn't. Maybe he'd been too angry to remember to do it.

Or too afraid.

Scowling, he focused on the thickest of the three books about Pets.

Two hours later, the scowl was more deeply etched into his face, and he threw the book aside in disgust.

People really did regard Pets entirely too much like dogs or cats – or dolls. He didn't care about proper feeding or treatment or punishing without marring. He wanted to know why Ruthven was asleep and when he would wake up, and if his blood had been contaminated with something that had caused Ruthven harm.

Snarling and muttering in frustration, he cast the Pet books on the floor and snatched up the history of vampires.

He did not recognize the name of the printer, or the publisher – plenty suspicious in its own right. He would bet every pence of his allowance that the book had been printed illegally. It was old, but well-cared for. He wondered how much it had cost his mother to purchase, and if his father knew she had it.

Except the last question was abruptly answered for him, like a blow to the gut, as he saw the inscription on the first page.

To my beauties, and our quest for answers and freedom ~Jonathan

Aubrey threw the book across the room, unable to bear what he was seeing.

His father had not simply known about his mother's struggle to free Pets – he had been part of it!

No, he refused to accept that. His strict, unbending, unreasonable father could not have been involved in a struggle to free Pets. He had not even had a Pet back then.

Shoving the thoughts aside, absolutely refusing to solve the infuriating riddle that his father was proving to be, Aubrey returned to the books about Pets and Pet care, hoping vainly that one of them would provide the answer he sought.

He read until it began to strain his eyes, and finally stood up to stretch and light the lamps, and ring for food.

When the food came, he ate it in bed, too impatient and in need of distraction to even think of stopping for longer than he already had.

He was so enthralled in the books, the hand upon his shoulder made him jump and yelp. Jerking around, he stared wide-eyed at a wide awake and grinning Ruthven. "What—

you—how—damn it!" Aubrey cast his book aside and shoved hard, sending Ruthven tumbling off the bed.

"Uncalled for," Ruthven said, slowly pulling himself to his knees and propping his arms on the bed, looking up at Aubrey with a wounded expression. "Why did you do that, master?" Slowly he climbed back onto the bed, as if wary of being shoved off again.

Aubrey was sorely tempted, and snapped, "Don't 'master'. You've been asleep for more than two days, and I've been worried sick, and you didn't even have the decency to-to-apologize or something, you just *grin* you infuriating bastard and I thought you were going to die so—"

He was cut off by Ruthven's mouth as it covered his own, so taken by surprise he did not even think to resist or pull away. Even when he recovered himself, he could not seem to make himself pull away. Ruthven tasted faintly of blood, but it wasn't as unpleasant as Aubrey would have thought, and he tasted of other things, which Aubrey could not quite place. His mouth was warm, lips soft, and wholly against his will Aubrey clung and let himself be thoroughly kissed.

"I'm sorry, master, I did not mean to worry you," Ruthven said softly when they finally broke apart.

His voice restored some of Aubrey's sense, and he ignored the way his face went hot at the knowledge he'd just let his damned Pet kiss him. "That is not good enough, damn it," he said. "You—" he stopped, not certain what to say, and simply glared. "Bastard."

"I'm very sorry, master," Ruthven said. "I never meant to cause you this much distress."

Aubrey narrowed his eyes, and realized Ruthven still held him. "Let me go," he said stiffly.

Ruthven smiled faintly, then leaned forward and kissed him again, tugging sharply when Aubrey tried to pull away, and then he was all but devouring Aubrey's mouth, destroying all attempts at protest, and how the hell had a Pet learned to kiss so well when he'd never belonged to anyone before?

Except he rather suspected Ruthven belonged to no one but himself, and had never been nor ever would be a proper Pet.

He moaned softly as the kiss deepened, letting himself be consumed by it, ignoring for now those parts of him screaming in protest. Arms slid around him, warm and solid, and Aubrey went with only a whimper when he was pulled down atop Ruthven.

Ruthven's hair was soft and thick, finer than even the fur throws he often used to beat back the cold. The body beneath his was solid and hard, far from unpleasant to be sprawled upon, even with the awkwardness of clothes between them.

"You always taste sweet, master," Ruthven said.

The sound of his voice brought Aubrey back to his senses, but even as he started to protest, Ruthven bit down on his bottom lip. The pain was bright and sharp, and briefly knocked his sense away again, and the slow drag of Ruthven's tongue across the wound ruined any chance of his sense returning.

"Intractable Pet," he muttered before he was overtaken once more by a hungry kiss, the coppery taste of blood stronger than ever – and it was his own, a fact that made him shiver, or maybe that was a result of the hands stroking up and down his back slipping just beneath his shirt to rake lightly across his skin.

Ruthven nuzzled his cheek, his throat. "Mm, hungry, master."

Aubrey groaned, struggling to remind himself why this was a bad idea, to order Ruthven to cease, but all that came out was, "Then feed."

Not needing to be told twice, Ruthven sank his fangs into Aubrey's throat.

He jerked, hissing in pain, but the hands boldly caressing him were equally distracting, and Aubrey was caught in a storm of sensation, lost between the pleasure and the pain. His hips moved without permission, grinding his trapped cock against Ruthven's, begging for a release he could not quite find, clashing with the pain of his blood being drained away, the bruise he could already feel forming from the ferocity of the bite.

Then Ruthven grabbed his hips, bringing him down hard as he thrust up, sucking harder still and Aubrey screamed in surprise and release.

He felt dizzy and sated as he collapsed on Ruthven, and so heavy with sleep he half wondered if he'd been drugged.

A warm tongue lapped at his throat, and he shivered at the sensation.

Rolling off Ruthven, he mustered enough energy to prop up on his elbows and glare at his Pet. "This was not supposed to happen."

"You should sleep, master. It is obvious you've not gotten proper rest while I slept. Again, I apologize most humbly."

Aubrey snorted, but was too tired to do anything but collapse into his pillows and mutter a reply. "You are wholly incapable of being humble about anything."

Ruthven laughed softly. "Yes, master."

He should get up and get cleaned, Aubrey thought sleepily. If he remained as he was, when he woke up he would be in agony.

But moving was too difficult an endeavor, and his bed was warm and comfortable even if his clothes were not, and the sound of Ruthven moving was, despite his efforts not to find it so, reassuring.

Tired of arguing with himself, Aubrey gave up and let sleep take him.

Musk Plant

(chapter nine)

There were precious places in which Stregoni felt comfortable. Of those few places, the apothecary was by far where he felt most at home.

It was as familiar to him as his reflection. From the time he was a boy he had been set simple chores within it, and once he was old enough to be trusted, he began to learn the ways of the various plants and powders, tinctures and potions. It was here he had learned the art of healing, and that sometimes healing meant hurting, and that there was a fine line between poison and cure.

Only once had he explored on his own, and he would never forget his mother's face, his father's quiet, as he was ill for days and weak for months.

It was also where his happiest memories were stored – cleaning the floor while his parents stocked the shelves and mixed medicines, laughing and joking and exchanging kisses when they thought he wasn't looking.

The smell of the flowers, the more pungent herbs, the bitter unguents and some of the just plain gross tinctures. People coming and going at all hours, some bright and cheerful, others hassled and angry, some red-faced with embarrassment...

He was not his father, or his grandfather, and people never really let him forget it – but enough saw him for himself, and said he would be great one day, and was nearly that now. He was young, yet, to be the primary doctor on hand – but he was better liked than the others in town, or so he was always told.

In the back, he could just hear his mother call that she was going next door for a bit. Calling back a reply, he resumed cleaning the counters until it gleamed in the afternoon sunlight pouring through the window. A rare reprieve, that sunlight, and the only reason he had been able to make it hope a couple of days ago.

Soon he would be going back to Sangre Manor, since the majority of his winter was always spent with Carmilla, studying the elusive disease which kept her weak and sickly. If he could just figure it out...

Shaking his head, he put away his rags and checked that his hair was still secured. That done, he washed his hands and then began to pull out the various ingredients and tools he would need to make a fresh batch of the various potions, tinctures, tonics, and ointments that were always in demand during the cold months.

He whistled as he worked, enjoying himself despite the chill that permeated the room. Grinding down leaves in a pedestal, lost in concentration, he did not really hear the bell which chimed as someone opened the door.

The amused throat clearing he did hear, and looked up with a start. "Oh, Terry. Good afternoon. How's your mother? Come for her tincture?"

"Aye," Terry said lightly, sliding onto one of the stools always kept at the counter for people waiting on this or that medication, or as someone else was treated. "Take your time, though. I'm in no hurry to get back. Can't walk a step without tripping over some niece or nephew or harpy aunt."

Stregoni laughed, absently shoving back an errant curl before he combined the past just created with a waiting solution, stirring all together vigorously before corking the bottle and setting it aside. "Your turn to put them all up, eh? They didn't all go having more babies, did they?"

"Oh, aye," Terry said with a long suffering sigh. "My mother and aunts want a hundred or more grandchildren, I think. They keep demanding why I'm not contributing to the count."

Laughing again, Stregoni began to pull down various selections from the mass of herb bundles hanging from the ceiling, combining them in seeming haphazard fashion, keeping track of everything even as he chatted aimlessly with Terry.

Terry with four aunts and five sisters, and more relatives than he could stand to count. They all took turns hosting the family during the winter months, a tradition common in most families.

It always made Stregoni feel a bit left out, that he had no family to share such a tradition. His mother had never been able to have more children, much to the dismay of his parents.

"So where do you put them all?" he asked as Terry continued to grouse about nieces and nephews.

"In my room," Terry said sourly, but with a faint smile that took any real ire from the words. "I'm about ready to sleep with the horses, if it'll get me a full night's rest. I envy you, my friend, this whole house just you and your mum. Must be nice."

Stregoni smiled. "Well, when it's quiet. As often as not, I'm woken at the oddest hours for one emergency or another. Sometimes, company would be nice."

"Well, if you ever want company, I'm more than happy to oblige," Terry said with a wink.

"I'll keep it in mind," Stregoni said, realizing with a start Terry was flirting.

He looked again, and sure enough – it wasn't just a dread of nieces and nephews keeping Terry sitting at the counter.

Stregoni resumed his work, abruptly realizing he'd stopped.

Not that he was interested, not really...but it was a nice change to be smiled and winked at. Flirting alone was a nice change. Gille—

He swallowed, cursing silently that his thoughts had gone precisely where he did not want them to go. Gille didn't flirt. Gille didn't wink – he didn't even smile. Yet between Terry's smiles, and Gille's stormy, unfathomable looks, there was simply no contest.

Stregoni wondered what that said about him.

"Here, now," Terry said, breaking into his thoughts. "Did I cause offense?"

"What?" Stregoni said, head jerking up. "Oh, no. Far from it. I'm sorry, my thoughts wandered down an unpleasant path." He forced a smile, willed thoughts of Gille to leave him the hell alone. "If you want to hide out more often, you must know you're welcome to linger here as long as you like." He shrugged. "I'm rarely here, of course, but that does not mean you cannot be. My mother would like the company, and she's always thought you a good sort."

Terry only smiled.

Stregoni smiled back, and finished off what he was working on, before pulling down more herbs to begin the next round. "So what else are you doing today?" he asked congenially, maybe flirting back a little bit, because there was no harm in flirting, and it was a pleasant surprise that someone might want to flirt with him.

Nothing would come of it, of course, but it wasn't a bad way to pass the afternoon for either of them.

An hour or two had passed when he finally finished the bulk of his work, and he finally pulled down what he needed to make up the tincture for which Terry had come in the first place. Stirring it all together, he carefully funneled it into a delicate-looking blue glass bottle. Placing the stopper, he slid it across the counter, bracing on his folded arms as they talked about the weather and a small soiree to which Terry had to escort a sister.

Stregoni startled when Terry abruptly reached out and caught up a stray curl of Stregoni's hair. "My sisters envy your hair, you know. 'All those copper curls' they say, going on and on. It really is—"

He paused as the door slammed open, turning around to see who had entered so noisily.

Of all the people Stregoni had thought to see today, it was not Gille.

His heart hammered in his chest as Gille stalked toward them, and there was no other word for the way he moved. Like a cat stalking a bird.

"Gille—"

Whatever he was about to say died as Gille reached out with a snarl and yanked Terry to his feet, then all but threw him toward the door. "Get out," he said, the words angry and sharp, brooking no argument.

Mouth agape, more than a little afraid, Terry turned and bolted.

Stregoni clenched his fists in fury. "What in the hell do you think you're doing, Gille?"

Gille only gave him a nasty, furious glare, then turned and stalked to the door which Terry had left hanging open. Slamming it shut, he flipped the sign to 'closed' and pulled down the shade, yanking the curtains over the picture window hastily shut before he stalked back across the room.

"The better question, Carrot, is what do you think you're doing?"

"Working," Stregoni hissed, slamming one hand down on the counter, leaning forward angrily. "You just threw out a good customer."

"Customer? For what services?" Gille demanded, his tone making it perfectly clear what he thought Terry had been seeking to purchase. "You were all but panting for him, Doctor. I didn't know you sold such things here."

Stregoni's face burned. "I do no such thing, you goddamn bastard! How dare you imply I am a whore. It's none of your business, anyway." He drew back, resisting an urge to throw something, but only barely. "Get the hell out of my shop."

"No," Gille said.

He stood in shock as Gille gripped the counter and neatly leapt over it. Stumbled back as Gille prowled toward him, swearing softly when he realized he'd only trapped himself between Gille and the wall.

"Go the hell away," he snarled, but could not miss the edge of desperation in his own voice.

"No," Gille repeated.

Stregoni flinched as Gille reached for him, and went still from shock when instead of whatever he'd expected, Gille only sank a hand into his curls, dislodging the ribbon holding them back, carding through them.

"What—"

"If you were desperate for attention, Carrot," Gille said in his mocking tone, "all you had to do was say."

Stregoni glared at him, even as he tried not to lean in to the touch of those hands, the way they sorted through his curls as though it were natural, when he knew for a fact Gille never bothered with his hair save to hold Stregoni where he wanted him. "I'll never be so desperate as that," he hissed, even though they both knew he was lying.

Gille smirked, then abruptly tightened his grip in Stregoni's hair and yanked him close, other arm like a band around Stregoni's waist. Then Gille was kissing him hard and Stregoni felt his lip split with the fury of it.

He struggled futilely in Gille's hold, but the bastard was having none of that, merely shifted to shove him against the counter, hand digging into his hip, and Stregoni knew he'd have bruises there.

When the kiss broke, he attempted to gasp out an angry protest, but the hand in his hair moved down to stroke the back of his neck in a way that turned Stregoni's gasp into a needy moan, and he hated himself, he really did, for always giving in so goddamn easily.

Gille took his mouth again, shoving a thigh between his legs, pressing hard, making Stregoni groan and move, beg for more with sound and body.

He broke away from the kiss only with the greatest of effort. "Why—"

A hard nip to his ear made the question fly from his thoughts.

"Do you honestly think that stupid clerk could give you what you want, Carrot?" Gille demanded, voice rough as he bit down harder on the soft skin below Stregoni's ear, sucking up a lurid mark.

Stregoni fisted his hands in the fabric of Gille's jacket. "None. Of. Your. Business—damn it!" He held fast despite himself as his breeches were undone, and Gille shoved a hand inside to pull out his cock, stroking with a familiarity Stregoni loved and hated in equal measure.

Then just as suddenly the hand was gone, leaving Stregoni gasping in surprise and dismay.

He got another hard kiss, his split lip throbbing now. "You must have something of use in here, Doctor."

"What?" Stregoni said, blinking uncomprehendingly – then the smug amusement on Gille's face made him realize. "No," he hissed. "You are not—"

Gille grabbed his hair and yanked his head back, kissing him dizzy, leaving him reeling, breathless, slumped against the counter desperate to stay standing and not give in to the way his knees wanted to give out.

He was alone for only a moment, as Gille vanished to explore the apothecary – and Stregoni wondered that he found what he sought so quickly, but didn't have time to think about it as the scent of yellow roses filled the room.

"Stop it—" But his words were cut off by a kiss, and his struggled to get away were futile – and, if he felt like being honest, half-hearted at best. Gille had him, and they both knew it, as sour and bitter a pill it was to swallow.

The cold air washed over him as his clothes were shoved out of the way, two slick fingers wasting no time in pushing inside him, twisting and stretching, and Stregoni was helpless to do anything but cling as Gille had his way.

He always had his way.

Stregoni groaned, fingers digging deep into Gille's arms as two became three, making him writhe. "Bastard—"

The fingers withdrew, and damn it this was not happening in his apothecary – his sanctuary, goddamn it.

But it was happening, there was no denying it. Stregoni groaned loud and long, head falling back, as Gille lifted him just so and pushed inside, sinking in slowly until he was fully seated.

Gille kissed him, deep and thorough, ravaging his mouth as he began to move – slowly at first, but with increasing fervor, until it was impossible to think of anything but the mouth upon his, the scents of velvet and lace, sweat and musk, mixed dizzyingly with the herbal, medicinal odors of the apothecary.

At some point, he realized hazily, his own fingers had done away with the silk ribbon binding back Gille's hair. He held on to it for dear life as Gille took him, thrust hard again and again, until Stregoni could no longer bear it and his scream of release was only just barely muffled in time by Gille's mouth.

Reality returned slowly, and yet all too quickly. He winced as Gille pulled out of him, and he was slowly lowered again to the floor. He wasn't certain his legs would hold, but they did.

Gille bent to retrieve his lost ribbon, and when he stood again he was nearly perfect – only his lips, wet and kiss swollen, the flush exertion had given his cheeks, gave away that they had done anything at all.

He looked away, shame overtaking him with the return of his senses.

But there was anger too, and it was that which brought his head back up. "Goddamn it, Gille – not here! Anyone could have—"

Gille kissed him, an edge to it that left Stregoni feeling like a man lost at sea. "Do not let me catch you doing such things again, Carrot."

Stregoni glared and shoved him back hard. "Who are you to tell me what I may or may not do?" He demanded. "I'm allowed to flirt where I please – to do whatever I please, with whomever."

With a snarl, Gille yanked him close, crushing his mouth all over again, until Stregoni could not remember the rest of what he'd wanted to shout about.

"No, you are not," Gille said when they broke apart again.

Stregoni stared at him, love and hate and longing and shame roiling in his stomach, lodging in his throat. "So what?" he asked bitterly. "I'm only allowed to be your whore, is that it?"

"That's right," Gille said. "Remember it – or else."

With that, Gille gathered up his things and left as suddenly as he had appeared.

Stregoni waited until he knew Gille was well and truly gone, then sank to the and buried his face in his arms, and sobbed.

It was only the realization, some time later, that his mother could return at any moment that forced him to his feet. With an effort, he dragged himself to his bedroom, quickly stripping out of his ruined clothes, washing off in the basin near his bed, scrubbing until his skin was red and raw and no traces of Gille remained.

Refreshed, dressed, ignoring the twinges of pain that were beginning to flare up, he returned to the apothecary.

The smell of sex was strong, making his cheeks heat with mortification – and perhaps a little more, because as much as he hated himself for it, there was no denying that he would never be capable of refusing Gille.

He just wished...

Shaking his head, he fetched water and soap and rags, and scrubbed and cleaned until the scent of sex was gone, until he could not longer smell the yellow roses which infused the oil Gille had used to—

Swearing, he put the cleaning things away again and went to fetch his *Pharmacopeia* and the various notes he had yet to transcribe, pulling up a barstool to work at the counter – which reminded him suddenly that the curtains were still drawn, and the sign still said closed.

Wincing slightly, for Gille had not been terribly gentle, he went and set all to rights, then returned to the counter.

He was just sitting down when the glint of jewels caught his eyes, and he slid off the barstool again to kneel on the floor, retrieving the glittering object.

A cravat pin – it had to belong to Gille. A fleur-di-lis made of diamonds and sapphire, set in silver.

Stregoni wrapped his hand around it, gripping it so tightly he could feel the hard jewels digging into his palm.

Then he tucked it away in his jacket, and bent to his work, losing himself to the comfortable familiarity of solving other people's problems.

Reeds

(chapter ten)

Aubrey looked up from glaring at his tea as the door opened, ready with sharp words should his father dare to intrude in his salon, far from certain what to say if Ruthven bothered him – but his mouth closed with a snap as he realized it was only Stregoni.

"You look as though you would like to take someone's head," Stregoni said with cautious humor. "I'm glad you decided not to take mine."

"I want to kill my father," Aubrey said sourly, finishing his tea and pouring more, motioning for Stregoni to help himself.

Stregoni dropped down in the armchair on the other side of the table which held the tea things, propping his feet up on an ottoman, unconsciously mimicking Aubrey' slouched, sulking posture. "Well, that is nothing new. What has he does now?"

Taking a sip of tea, Aubrey related the shouting match of a few days ago, in his father's room, the revelation of what his parents had once done – the tongue lashing he had received when he'd attempted for a second time to confront his father about it.

"I woke up yesterday to discover that all materials pertaining to it had been taken from my room, and we near brought the breakfast room down around our feet shouting it out this morning," Aubrey concluded morosely. "The bastard is bound and determined to keep me from resuming the work they began, and he abandoned after my mother and Mina die. I don't get why! Surely the greatest revenge against the murderers, the greatest tribute to the memory of my mother and Mina, would be to reach their lost goal. Why is he so stubborn?"

Stregoni smiled faintly over the rim of his teacup. "Stubbornness does rather seem to be a family trait."

Aubrey shot him a suspicious look, but Stregoni only looked blandly back.

"Maybe he's scared," Stregoni continued, "that to resume the work would mean more deaths. He already lost his wife and lover—" He broke off, an odd expression on his face.

"Yeah," Aubrey said, knowing what he was thinking. "I was feeling the same way for days."

He was still feeling that way – his father had not directly confirmed it, but he hadn't directly denied it either, which was as good as a confirmation. His father hadn't just loved his mother, but also Mina – they all three of them—

Taking another sip of tea, Aubrey shook his head.

"Go, Lord Sangre," Stregoni muttered absently over his own tea.

Aubrey rolled his eyes.

"So," Stregoni said, "you're in here in sulking?"

"Essentially."

Stregoni grinned. "Sounds good to me. I'm due to make my regular visit to Blackfield. I do not know if I should make it or not, and deciding the matter is giving me a headache."

"If they are going to be right bastards," Aubrey said shortly. "I do not see why they are worth your time and effort.

The weather had cleared rather abruptly, but it could turn foul again at any moment. Why should you risk that for a family which did nothing but turn you out like some commoner?"

"I am a commoner," Stregoni said gently. "Anyway, I'm worried about Tony. That damned quack..."

Aubrey made soothing noises, nodding in acknowledgement. He could understand that – he would do anything to save Carmilla. He could not imagine being Stregoni, who must worry about hundreds of people.

He lit upon a sudden idea.

"I say, Stregoni, why don't I go with you?"

"What?"

"I'll go with you," Aubrey repeated, finishing his tea and setting the cup down with a clink and rattle. "My presence will scare them some, if only because it's impossible not to know my sire, and that will make them behave a bit more than they otherwise would – mayhap even let you examine tony." He clapped his hands once in sudden amusement. "I'll even drag Ruthven along, make it a proper 'I am the son of an earl and you'll do what I say' visit. If I have to be an earl's son, I may as well put it to some use."

Stregoni looked at him. "That's not like you, to have anything whatsoever to do with your father."

"Yes, well," Aubrey said. "If I'm going to pursue freeing Pets, I shall have to learn to use all my resources – unfortunately, that includes my role as heir." He made a face. "If my father does not disown me for defying him. How ironic that my new could result in my finally being disowned, and now it's the last thing I want."

"You do like to make things difficult, Brey," Stregoni said with a laugh. "How is Ruthven, by the way? No more relapses?"

"No," Aubrey replied, pointedly ignoring the look on his friends face. He slumped down in his chair. "I didn't mean for that to happen," he muttered guiltily, body going tight and hot as he remembered what had transpired after Ruthven had woken -- and though he was doing his damndest to avoid letting it happen again, Ruthven was more than happy to take intimate liberty now that he'd done it once.

Damned Pet.

He wondered if Ruthven would still want him were he free, for even if he was the oddest Pet that Aubrey had ever known, there was the simple fact he'd drunk Aubrey's blood. That was a tie even Ruthven couldn't overcome.

Surely.

Which reminded him the blood dependency would be an issue whenever Pets obtained freedom.

There were dozens upon dozens of issues, most of which he could probably clear up with his mother's notes, except of course his father had taken care of that.

"Have you heard a word I've said?"

"Huh?" Aubrey asked, snapping back to the present. "No, apologies. I was lost in thought."

Stregoni snorted. "Thinking about going to find your Pet?"

"No," Aubrey said hastily, ignoring Stregoni's laughter. "What were you saying?"

"That I should go check on Carmilla, then we can perhaps grab a quick supper and be on our way? If we leave soon enough, we can return same day instead of overstaying the lack of welcome we are sure to receive."

Aubrey nodded. "Sounds good to me. Let's check on Carmilla, then I'll go find Ruthven to inform him before we go scrounge dinner."

Stregoni smiled and set his down, standing with a flourish. "Come on then."

Taking more time to stand and adjust his clothes, Aubrey returned the smile and followed Stregoni from the room. "Where is Carmilla this time of day?" He pondered aloud.

"Beggin' pardon, my lord," a maid said nervously, from where she'd been polishing and dusting. "Her ladyship is always at her music lessons this hour. She should be in the music room."

"Thank you," Aubrey said with a smile.

Flushing bright, the maid bent back to her task.

Stregoni waited until they were well away. "Flirting with the staff now, are we?" He said, laughing and elbowing Aubrey.

"Shut up," Aubrey said, rolling his eyes. "You know me better than that."

"Yeah, yeah," Stregoni said, still snickering. "Come on, to the music room we go."

They walked in companionable silence, each lost to his own thoughts, occasionally exchanging glances, and Aubrey realized that none of his friends at school had been like Stregoni. Lords sons, all of them, and he had gotten along with them, and missed them – but they weren't Stregoni.

The Benefici family had always been close to Sangre, since their grandfathers had first met and gotten on together, no matter the impropriety of an Earl calling a mere doctor friend. Their fathers had been good friends as well...

Aubrey let out a soft chuff of laughter.

"What's so amusing?" Stregoni asked.

"I just realized you're one tradition I followed, so far as the Earls in my family are concerned."

Stregoni blinked at that, then laughed as he got it. "Well, if your honor demands we start up a feud in order to anger you father, I suppose—" He stopped abruptly, an odd look flickering across his face. Confusion, but also pain.

Aubrey frowned in concern. "Stregoni?"

"I know that tune..." Stregoni said.

"It's a fairly common one..." Aubrey said, but trailed off as he really listened to it himself. A sad piece, but that wasn't what struck him – it was that it was traditionally played by two people, and was being played by two people now.

Well, not so strange, really. Likely Carmilla's tutor was simply having them play a duet.

Stregoni still frowned beside him, and Aubrey had to take his arm and drag him a moment before he resumed walking.

He pushed open the door to the music room – and came to an abrupt halt.

Whatever he'd expected, it wasn't the sight before him.

Carmilla sat on the left side of the bench, long hair bundled only loosely, so the curls tumbled down her back in seeming haphazard fashion, decorated here and there with jeweled wood anemone. Her dress was ice blue, trimmed in silver and gold, shining in the light streaming through the windows.

The strange part was the way she occasionally looked up and smiled at her tutor as they played – and the way her tutor smiled back.

He hadn't known his damnable cousin could smile, especially with what suspiciously looked like sincerity.

Gille's hair was down too, as though neither one of them had thought any sort of formality necessary for the lesson. Even his afternoon jacket had been tossed aside, deep blue lace against the crimson velvet of the settee. He was beautiful and relaxed and almost friendly looking as they played the complicated duet, exchanging occasional friendly smiles.

As they finished, Carmilla clapped her hands and laughed in delight. "I did not falter once – I guess I can be taught."

"Of course you can, sweet," Gille said, reaching out to ruffle her loose curls. He reached out to take a sip from the brandy tumbler on a nearby table. "Now, let's play it one more time, then we'll move on to a new piece."

"Yes, Gille," Carmilla said obediently. Her fingers moved promptly back to the keys, beginning again the beautiful, haunting melody they had been playing earlier. After a moment, Gille joined in, and together the two played it through a second time, as flawlessly as they had the first.

Aubrey clapped when they finished, causing his sister to squeak and turn around, nearly knocking herself from the bench.

"Brey!" She said, smiling. "What do you think?"

He strode across the room and took her hands, kissing the knuckles. "I think you play as fine as any princess. Beautiful." His eyes slid to Gille, whose face had slid back into its perpetual expression of frozen, uncaring beauty. Aubrey almost thought he'd imagined the smiles Gille had so easily exchanged with Carmilla.

"What are you doing here?" Carmilla asked.

"We came to see how you were," Aubrey said, but further explanation fell away as he took in the strange look on Stregoni's face – Stregoni who was staring at Gille, who was clearly ignoring him.

He frowned, wondering what the devil was going on.

Carmilla's hands tightened on his own, and he looked back at his sister, who only gave a minute shake of her head. She kept hold of him with one hand, using the others to gather up her voluminous skirts with practiced ease, guiding him to the hallway.

Ignoring the more confusing matter of his friend for the moment, Aubrey voiced an easier question. "When did Gille start tutoring you in music?"

"Since he caught my tutor trying to make inappropriate advances," Carmilla said, voice level, as she smoothed her skirts back out.

"What!" Aubrey bellowed.

Carmilla looked at him in amusement. "Father took care of the matter."

"I should hope so," Aubrey snarled. "How dare the bastard—"

She laughed, interrupting his tirade before he could get started. "You know, Brey, I never noticed until this moment – you and father are a lot alike."

Aubrey narrowed his eyes. "There is no need to go about slinging insults, Milla."

Carmilla only laughed again.

He started to speak again when the door to the music room was abruptly thrown open, and Stregoni stumbled out looking as though he were about to either scream or cry. Aubrey stared. "Stregoni—"

"Carmilla," Stregoni said, then coughed to clear his throat, raising his voice to speak over the melody now pouring from the music room – deeper, sadder, and far more tempestuous than the bittersweet melody from before. No, this piece was almost wild, like an uncontrollable grief. Stregoni coughed again, trying in vain to get his voice to sound normal, and not as though he was choking on something. "I came to make certain you would be all right for a day or so, before I left to carry on my duties."

"You're leaving?" Carmilla said with a frown. "But you can't, what about supper?"

They both stared at her blankly. Aubrey shook his head. "What supper?"

Carmilla sighed in exasperation. "Honestly, does no one around here communicate? Did father not tell you that the Blackfields have been invited to dinner, and they are bringing their new personal physician with them." She slid a glance to Stregoni. "I say invited, but to be honest it was more they were ordered to come or else. Apparently they have many apologies to make, unless they want father to return the insult thrice over."

"What?" Stregoni said. "You can't mean me."

She reached up to kiss his cheek. "Of course you, silly. You are a dear friend of the family – no way would father tolerate such an insult."

"How the devil did father find out?" Aubrey asked.

Carmilla shrugged. "I believe Gille relayed the information to him, and father of course lost his temper, and then sent Gille out to issue the threats in person."

"W-what?" Stregoni asked. "Why would Gille do that?"

"He is part of this family, for all the lot of you seem intent upon killing each other." She shook her head, clucking soft disapproval. "Though, I concede Gille excels at being difficult."

"To say the least," Stregoni muttered. They fell silent briefly, listening to the heartbreaking sounds still pouring from the music room. "Bastard."

Carmilla frowned, but did not argue with him.

Aubrey looked at her. "How do you know so much, Milla?"

She gave him a smile that was sad and weary and faintly amused. "Brey, I spend my days on reading, writing, needlework, and music – and listening to everything which is happening around me. Today is the first time in a week I have been strong enough to be up and about, rather than confined to my rooms. I know what's going on around the house, because I will never know what goes on beyond it." She patted his cheek, then leaned up to kiss it softly, smelling like pink roses and chrysanthemums.

He kissed her cheek in return. "I do love you, little sister."

"I know," she said, and reached up to cup is face briefly in her pale, fragile-looking, not quite steady hands. "I love you too, Brey." She withdrew her hands and stepped away. "Now, I must go and get ready for supper, and I suggest you do the same, or you and father will no doubt have another row."

Stifling a sigh, for he'd been looking forward to escaping the house for a day or so, Aubrey nodded and dragged Stregoni with him, not even bothering to draw his haunted-looking friend into conversation before they split up to go their separate ways.

That riddle would have to wait until later tonight, or even tomorrow, depending on how the damned supper went.

Oleander

(chapter eleven)

Stregoni was still trembling as he reached his room, and gave in to a pathetic urge to slam his door shut.

Gille had been smiling – really smiling – at Carmilla.

He was used to being jealous of Francois, though that had eased since their strange encounter. But Carmilla – what did she do to earn smiles, when he would give up everything he had for just one.

Pressing the heels of his hands to his eyes, Stregoni willed all thoughts of the bastard away, scrubbing at his sore lips, where Gille had kissed him just to enrage him. There'd been no tenderness in it, just a...feverishness, and he was so very tired of trying to unravel the mystery that was Gille.

Sighing, he began to strip out of his casual clothing, pulling out what he would need for a more formal supper – which brought him right back to thoughts of Gille.

Damn it.

This supper could have nothing to do with him. Carmilla must be mistaken. Why would Gille and Lord Sangre go to this much trouble just because Stregoni had been slighted?

Well, if it was a matter of upsetting someone close to the family – which he was, there was little point in being modest about that – then of course honor and appearances and all must be preserved.

Somehow, the thought was disheartening. Fool him, he thought viciously, for wasting even a second thinking it might be something more than that. Gille had not been outraged on his behalf that day Stregoni had mistakenly wound up at his home – he'd been mad Stregoni was there at all. He'd probably wanted to know who was the cause of the interference.

Finding out it was someone who should know better simply meant the matter must be attended.

Sighing again, he moved to his mirror to attack his neck cloth, frowning in annoyance as he tied a seemingly simple, but ultimately complicated knot. When the good linen lay as it should, he rifled through his meager collection of jewelry for a pin. His fingers lingered on the fleur-di-lis he had yet to return to Gille, thumb rubbing the glittering jewels.

Realizing what he was doing, Stregoni scowled and dropped it, then finally chose a simple jonquil made from gold and silver. Fastening it in place, he gave his reflection a critical examination.

He still could not see what about him first made Gille decide to toy with him, and he certainly could not see anything that would ever gain him what he wanted, no matter how hard he tried to stop wanting it.

Feeling as ready as he ever would, smoothing down his blue-gray velvet dinner jacket, adjusting his breeches, he finally conceded he was as ready as he would ever be. He hated formal dinners, but if Lord Sangre wanted to make a point about something, then this dinner would be formal in the extreme – just to make everyone uncomfortable.

Except, of course, Lord Sangre and Gille, who did it naturally as breathing.

The dinner bell had not yet rung, and wouldn't for some time yet. Anxious to keep himself occupied, lest he do something stupid, Stregoni headed for the library. Pouring himself a brandy from the small bar there, he wandered through the collection for several minutes before finally selecting a history of medicine, and sat down to read in the chair closest to the fire.

He was, thankfully, left completely in peace until the dinner bell rang a couple of hours later. Closing the book, he tossed back the last of his brandy and strode from the library.

Only to be immediately struck by the image of Gille in formal dress – all black and white and silver, hair pulled neatly back, drawing the gaze immediately to his gold-flecked jade eyes. Jewels glistened at his throat, reminding Stregoni of the pin he knew he had no intention of returning. Tonight's pin was a simple diamond trefoil.

Stregoni looked away before Gille could catch him staring, and moved ahead of him to enter the salon where everyone was gathered. He looked around the room, and his gaze mistakenly locked with William's. The bastard still looked the same as ever – too rich, too cocky, to be a real doctor.

He deliberately looked away, refusing to be more polite that was strictly required.

"Stregoni, there you are," Lord Sangre said, from where he sat in a large chair, making it painfully clear he was lord of the manor. "Lord and Lady Blackfield have been speaking of you. Blackfield, my lady, Doctor Benefici."

"Doctor," Blackfield said formally, if a bit stiffly. "We have come to apologize for the behavior we exhibited several days ago. It was unseemly."

They really were here because they'd mistreated him. Stregoni could not fathom it – the people he helped were often unpleasant. Everyone wanted an instant remedy, a quick cure, and fear often turned them mean and angry when they did not get it – especially when they knew there would never be a cure. It was part of his job. No one had ever really apologized before, not like this.

"Of course," he said. "You are worried for poor Tony. How is he?"

"Not well," Lady Blackfield said miserably. "As sick as ever, it does not matter what we try."

Lord Sangre stirred. "I am certain Stregoni can make time to go see him, if you are agreeable."

"Of course," Lady Blackfield murmured. "We were of course hasty, in our distress."

"Of course," Sangre repeated, but Stregoni knew the glint in his eye. "Stregoni, you could perhaps make time to return with them tomorrow?"

"Yes, my lord," he replied, hoping that the implied 'thank you' was understood.

From the nod he received, it clearly was.

"Gille," Sangre said. "Ring for the port and sherry. Elisabeth, my dear, play us something on your harp. Ah, Carmilla, there you are, and your brother with you."

Carmilla curtsied as she entered. "Yes, father. I waylaid Aubrey, and made him help me down the stairs."

Sangre nodded. "Lord Blackfield, my lady, you of course remember my son and heir, Aubrey. I believe you've met Carmilla before as well."

The introductions continued, and eventually William was drawn forward into the fray, to make his own apologies. Contrite as the words sounded, there was no way for Stregoni to miss the hate and rage that sparked in William's eyes.

Whatever had transpired since he had been thrown out of Blackfield manor, William hated him for it.

Stregoni murmured a polite acceptance, stifling a sigh of relief when William once more vanished into the background, and polite chit chat continued haltingly until the bell finally rang again, signaling that dinner was ready.

Lord Sangre murmured for the Pets to remain and enjoy themselves, then led the little dinner party from the salon.

They filed into the great dining room, which was lit with a profusion of candles in ornate candelabra, the table itself set with a good silk cloth, and more candles interspersed with bouquets of yellow lilies and peonies.

Of course he would wind up sitting directly across from Gille, Stregoni thought miserably. William was to his left, Aubrey to his right, giving him one ally against two foes – or a foe and whatever the hell Gille was, because foe seemed to simple a word for the way his stomach was roiling in misery at how devastating Gille looked in candlelight.

Swallowing, Stregoni fought an urge to down the contents of his wineglass in one go. His head was already spinning enough, thanks to the brandy from the library and port from the salon.

His attempts at making the best of the situation by conversing with William only earned him perfunctory replies. He was not stupid enough to try and converse with Gille, and so settled on chatting with Aubrey, whenever poor Brey was not locked in conversation with his father and the Blackfields.

As he'd known, the only two completely comfortable were Lord Sangre and Gille, who moved through the routines of dinner like hungry sharks. Carmilla looked vaguely amused, but also tired.

Stregoni resisted an urge to offer to take her upstairs, feeling guilty that he would use her as an excuse to get himself out of this miserable situation.

He stifled another sigh as the first course was finally served, barely hiding a grimace as William fumbled with the serving tray and utensils, nearly upsetting the whole thing. Normally he would sympathize, for he'd very nearly done that very thing himself more than once – but the bastard was not even putting a good face on things, and Stregoni was already half-drunk and gloomy. Let him suffer. He'd feel guilty for being spiteful later.

The food was, as always, perfect. He would never tell his mother so, but his favorite place to eat was right here – though he preferred the more casual dinners that were usually just he and Aubrey, sometimes Carmilla, very rarely Gille and Sangre, who ate at a different hour, or simply a different place. More and more often now, Ruthven shadowed their meals, and it was increasingly amusing to see how much the Pet affected Aubrey.

Unfortunately, such amusements were not available tonight, and Stregoni knew he was drinking far too much but could not be bothered to stop.

He looked up, far too weak to resist any longer, drinking in the sight of a man too beautiful and cold to ever belong to him. It was beyond his comprehension why he had what he did – stolen, midnight moments of wild passion, that damned moment in his apothecary.

Gille shifted his gaze, and caught Stregoni staring, and he knew the bastard was smirking even if his mouth was still curved in a polite smile. He could see it in the eyes, that Gille knew all too well the nature of Stregoni's thoughts.

Jerking his gaze away, he made another miserable attempt to get William to stop being such an ass.

When the whole wretched affair finally drew to a close, he could not escape fast enough, but bolted as quickly as his alcohol-addled limbs permitted to his chambers. His clothes had long ago grown stifling, and he stripped down hastily to just his breeches and shirt, shucking his buckled shoes and collapsing face down on top of his bed, too tired and drained to be bothered to do anything else.

He was jerked away by the sound of a hoarse scream, a shout, the sound of something breaking, crashing, and was out of his door before he was entirely awake.

The sound—his pace increased as he realized the horrific sounds were coming from Gille's chambers.

Just as he reached for the door, it flew open, clipping him on the side of the head as he failed to move quickly enough. His protests died in his throat, however, as Gille and Francois stumbled out, locked in some terrible struggle.

The smell of blood was strong, and Stregoni stared in horror as he realized it was because Gille was covered – soaked – in blood.

With another shout, of anger and pain and fear, Gille threw Francois off.

Stregoni recoiled, stumbling back, catching the open door to keep from falling entirely, as he stared wide-eyed at Francois.

The Pet was like nothing he'd ever seen – his eyes were wide, crazed, and he was smeared with blood from mouth to chest. As though...

Oh, god.

He looked down at Gille, who abruptly lay far too still on the floor. Just as he knelt, however, a snarl brought his head sharply back up and he barely threw himself out of the way as Francois lunged for him, scrambling to his feet as the Pet recovered and came at him again.

Letting out a panicked shout of his own, part of his mine still firmly with the unconscious Gille, Stregoni struggled to stay away from whatever the hell Francois had become – and ran straight into someone else, sending them both tumbling to the cold marble tile of the hallway landing.

He scrambled to sit up, and realized with a shock that he had crashed into William.

"What is going on?" William demanded. "I heard—"

Francois' wild snarls cut him off, and he stared in wide-eyed horror.

"Get up, get up," Stregoni said, standing and pulling William up – but William was frozen with panic, and Stregoni bolted away at the last as Francois came at them.

William moved, but too late, struggling against the crazy Pet, screaming loudly in panic, shrieking as Francois bit into him.

Then he tripped, and they both went tumbling back, all the way down the main staircase.

Stregoni turned away, not bothering to see where and how they landed, his heart hammering in his chest as one thought and one thought alone consumed him – Gille.

He lay far too still, and Stregoni saw immediately why there was so much blood. Francois had bit him hard and deep, and in the struggle which had clearly erupted, there had been no time to heal the wound.

Too much blood. Tears stung his eyes even as he moved to stop the flow of blood, refusing to admit that far too much of it had soaked into Gille's clothes, into the costly rugs.

"Stregoni!"

He looked up, eyes blurry, and could just make out the moonlit figure of Aubrey – and Ruthven, he realized, was just behind him.

"Too much blood," Stregoni managed. "Francois attacked him, but he's lost—"

Ruthven made a sound that almost sounded like a growl as he knelt beside Stregoni, reaching out to touch Gille, a frown etched deep into his handsome face.

"What in the hell is going on?" Aubrey said.

Stregoni started to answer, but his voice was drowned out by the resumption of noise from below, the voices of the others as they came to investigate the noise. He ignored them, unable to focus on anything but the man lying too still and pale before him.

"Master," Ruthven said, drawing Aubrey away from where he'd been talking with his father, Lord Blackfield, who vanished to go see what had become of the two downstairs. "Master," Ruthven repeated. "I can save him, but I need your help."

Aubrey dropped down opposite them. "What in the hell are you talking about?"

"Trust me," Ruthven said softly.

They stared at each other for what must have been an eternity, but surely was only a moment.

"All right," Aubrey said, voice just as soft.

Barely had he spoken the words when Ruthven moved, closing the space between them, burying his fangs in Aubrey's throat.

Aubrey let out a startled cry of pain, but did nothing more than cling to Ruthven for balance.

Ruthven tore away after a moment, then lifted Gille up and closed his mouth around the wound that was more on his shoulder than in his throat – so Francois had not quite gotten the bite for which he'd been aiming, but still...

What was going on?

Twice Ruthven repeated the strange process of feeding from Aubrey, then...whatever he was doing to Gille.

When he finally stopped, he slumped over with his eyes closed.

"Master," Ruthven said quietly. "I'm going to need to sleep for a day or two. Do not be alarmed. I think...his blood...poisoned..." Then he abruptly fell forward, Aubrey barely catching him in time to avoid crushing Gille.

Together they fumble awkwardly to separate the two unconscious men.

Stregoni looked down at Gille – he was still far too pale, but he was obviously breathing, and the awful wound was closed up. Nearby, Aubrey was just as intent upon Ruthven.

They shared a look, then looked away again. He should move Gille to bed, Stregoni thought distantly, but he simply could not muster the energy.

He looked up at the sound of footsteps, and saw Lord Sangre approach them, mouth draw in a tight line. Lord Blackfield trailed behind him, anger and guilt and shame on his face.

"Francois is dead," Lord Sangre said. "We can find no sign of William."

Stregoni shook his head, unable to form words.

"What's going on?" Aubrey asked. "Ruthven said something about poison."

Lord Sangre looked furious, but it was a still, cold fury – the worst possible kind, Stregoni knew. It was better for all when he simply lost his temper. When he got like this....

"I do not know," Lord Sangre said. "I intend to find out. How are they?"

"Fine," Stregoni said. "They both likely will sleep for several days."

"I thought Ruthven was fine only a moment ago," Lord Sangre said with a frown, but he held up a hand when Stregoni and Aubrey both fumbled to answer. "Explanations can wait. For now, let us get them to bed, then begin to sort out this mess. Brey, go find your sister and assure her that all is well."

Stregoni felt numb. "Francois is really dead?"

Lord Sangre nodded, then turned away to summon servants to begin cleaning up the various messes.

Blue Convolvulus

(chapter twelve)

Aubrey groaned, eyes fluttering as he battled sleep to stay conscious. Groaning again, he slowly found purchase and struggled to sit up.

"Stay still," said a gentle voice, and after a moment he realized it was Stregoni in doctor mode.

He grunted and ignored the command – but it took it more slowly after a wave of dizzy promptly dropped him back down upon the bed. "What—where—Streg, what's going on?"

"You've been asleep a little over a day," Stregoni said.

That he remembered – well, passing out he sort of remembered. Whatever Ruthven had done, by the end of it all Aubrey had felt weak as a baby. Only his refusal to drop before Ruthven was safely in their bed had kept him from passing out sooner.

He slowly turned his head to look at Stregoni, who was slumped tiredly on a stool pulled close to the bed.

"You look exhausted," he said, immediately feeling guilty. Of course it would be Stregoni who took care of them all. Then everything came rushing back to him. "Ruthven. Gille. How are they?"

Not waiting for a reply, he turned to look at the other half of the bed, relief undoing the knot in his chest as he saw that Ruthven looked no different than the last time he'd gone into a deep sleep.

"Ruthven is fine," Stregoni said, yawning. "Gille is sleeping at least as hard, but seems okay otherwise." He frowned.

That drew Aubrey's attention to something else he'd noted during the awful night. "Stregoni...how long have you been in love with Gille?" Because there was no mistaking the way Stregoni had looked bent over an unconscious and – at the time – very likely dead Gille.

Stregoni flinched at the question, and did not reply.

Aubrey didn't press it, not really able to comprehend it, and still too tired to try and figure it out.

"Carmilla is not getting any better," Stregoni said.

"Milla?" Aubrey said, snapped from where he'd turned back to Ruthven. "What's wrong with Milla?"

Stregoni shook his head. "I don't know. She's been sick since last night – I think the shock and the fear were too much for her frail body. She is sleeping, as well." He sighed and rubbed his forehead tiredly, and the shadows beneath his eyes suddenly looked all the worse.

"What time is it?" Aubrey asked.

"Coming on eight o'clock," Stregoni said, smiling weakly. "I was beginning to think the lot of you would sleep forever. Your father is downstairs in his study. Blackfield and his wife are confined to their rooms until Lord Sangre sees fit to let them return home. He is, to say the least, quite furious with them. We still cannot find William. Elisabeth managed to confirm for us that we were, indeed, poisoned – but it seems to be a poison which affects just Pets."

Aubrey frowned. "That makes no sense. What is the point?"

Stregoni shrugged. "I do not know. If your father has figured something out, he has not said." He stood up slowly, grasping the bed for balance.

"You are dead on your feet," Aubrey said, sliding slowly from the bed himself. "Go rest, Streg. You will probably be needed later, so it's better that you rest now. I can manage until you wake, just tell me what to do."

"Nothing," Stregoni said. "Keep an eye on your sister, make her drink her tonic whenever she stirs. Try to make your father sleep. Check on Gille, but he should be fine, I think. Whatever your odd Pet did, he will be fine once he wakes."

Aubrey shifted his gaze to Ruthven, fast asleep and perfectly still, like some exotic doll stretched out on his bed. "Yes, my odd Pet. That is still another question that will require an answer at a later date."

Likely his father would be bellowing for those very answer. Stifling a sigh, Aubrey took Stregoni by the arm and all but dragged him from the room and towards his own – but he hesitated halfway there, remembering the look upon Stregoni's face when he thought Gille would die.

He did not understand it. His cousin was a bastard of the highest order...but there was no mistaking that look, and Stregoni was more his brother than his friend. If there were answers to be had about the oddity of it, he would get them later.

Changing directions, he guided Stregoni to Gille's door.

"What?" Stregoni said, struggling to break free. "I don't think—"

"Just go rest," Aubrey said, opening the door and pushing him inside.

When Stregoni did not move, he pushed him toward and onto the bed.

"This is a bad idea," Stregoni said, looking around the richly appointed room as though he expected something to leap out and bite him. Then his eyes landed on Gille, and he forgot to keep struggling. "He'll kill me," he said softly.

Aubrey snorted. "I doubt Gille will be capable of fluffing his own pillow when he wakes. You're worried about him, so stay here and keep an eye on him. I'll be busy with other things. Tug the bell pull if there's a problem."

He did not wait for a reply, but strode from the room, closing the door firmly behind him.

In the hallway, he had to rest a bit, wait for the world to steady beneath him.

First thing was first – he needed to get cleaned up and changed, then find food.

Then...then he would have to go and speak with his father, and see what the two of them could figure out, as there was simply no one else to do it.

He returned to his bedroom and fumbled to pull out fresh clothes, ringing for a servant. Turning away from his wardrobe, his gaze landed absently on the window.

Outside, the snow had resumed falling – and it looked as though it had been falling for some time, and rather heavily. Just a few days ago it had begun to melt. Now they were once more being consumed by winter. The moonlight made all the snow glow, where it slipped through between the heavy clouds.

It was, he thought, rather like being caught in a dream.

He turned and looked at Ruthven.

Perhaps nightmare was the more accurate term.

Hearing the servant arrive, he bundled his clothes together and went to order a bath and food.

Two hours later, he wanted only to go back to bed. Another pot of tea would take care of the worst of the exhaustion, but he still would rather linger here and make certain Ruthven would be all right.

"What are you?" he asked softly, brushing back a strand of Ruthven's hair. It was as eerie now as it had been the first time Ruthven had gone into a deep sleep.

Exertion, that was obviously the reason behind it. But what had Ruthven done the first time to exhaust himself? Hell, he still wasn't certain he knew what Ruthven had done this time. Saved Gille by taking Aubrey's blood – that's what it seemed like, anyway.

Shaking his head, allowing himself one more glance at his too-still Pet, Aubrey turned away and left his rooms.

Downstairs, he knocked on the door to his father's study, then pushed the door opened when he heard something.

His father was sitting at his desk, for once not dressed to the hilt, but sitting in nothing more than his shirtsleeves, rolled up as he read through various books.

Books Aubrey knew he'd never seen before, and he was doubly sure of it when he drew enough to read the titles. "Where have these been?" he demanded.

Sangre looked up at him, tired and angry – but amused. "In my room," he said calmly. "Where sons with a tendency to defy me would not find them."

Aubrey glared, but could not muster the energy to be truly angry.

"You should still be resting," Sangre replied.

"So should you," Aubrey shot back. "What have you learned?"

Sangre set down a book he'd been reading, leaning back in his seat and scrubbing at his face tiredly. "Call for tea, would you?"

"I already told them to bring it here," Aubrey said. "Tell me."

"Patience, Brey," Sangre muttered. "I knew what was going on the moment the word poison came up." He sighed and picked up one of the books on his desk, rifling through the pages, then turned and pushed it toward Aubrey. "I believe poor Francois was killed by an extract made from the garlic flower," he said quietly. "I have seen its effect upon vampires only once before."

Aubrey startled, looking at his father. "What did you call them?"

"Vampires?" Sangre asked, mouth quirking in amusement. "Your mother and I never called Mina our Pet – she was always just a vampire to us. We believed, once, that half the battle was overcoming the Pet stigma, and that so long as they were called Pets, that was all they'd ever be."

Nodding, still not certain how to handle the fact his strict father had once fought to free Pets, Aubrey glanced down at the book. "Garlic flower?"

"Yes," Sangre said, still sounding far too amused. "Vampires are, for reasons unknown, highly allergic to all parts of the garlic plant. Usually, it's not a problem – humans do not ingest enough of it, on those occasions we do, to cause vampires real harm. Most are not even aware of the problem. Those that are, take care to feed their Pets well before or well after they have eaten. Even if they don't, the worst that happens is that the vampire takes sick for a little while. A case of vampire poisoning has not occurred in many years."

Aubrey frowned. "Why?" he asked. "I don't understand who would have done this, and why."

Sangre leaned back in his chair, and crossed his arms over his chest. "I think our culprit is William – that much is obvious by the way he has vanished. We will run him to ground, eventually. This weather hinders him as much as us. The why eludes me – I can only assume it has something to do with the fuss Gille and I raised over the way Stregoni was treated. A bit of an overreaction, which leads me to conclude William did not quite mean things to go as they did."

"Francois is dead," Aubrey said quietly. "I never cared for him, but he had nothing to do with this – what exactly happened?"

"He had enough garlic, ingested through the feeding, that it simply drove him crazy. It would have made him crave still more blood, in an attempt to find untainted food, but the more he ingested, the worse it became. He finally died from simply having taken in too much."

Aubrey closed his eyes. "I never thought I'd say it, but poor Gille. I might not have been fond of Francois, but I'm sure Gille was, after a fashion."

"You might try saying 'poor Gille' more often," his father said in a tone of quiet reprimand. "There is more to your cousin than you have ever bothered to learn." He grunted softly. "Though, that certainly goes both ways."

"If you say so," Aubrey said, but couldn't muster the will to really argue, not when he remembered Stregoni's face. For his best friend to feel that way...either Gille was more of a monster than he'd always believed, or far less of one.

He put the thought aside to deal with later, one more on what was going to be a very long list.

"How did Gille survive?" Sangre asked. "I saw him, before I went downstairs to find Francois and William. He should not be alive. Ruthven has fallen into his strange, deep sleep again -- I cannot think the two are unrelated."

Aubrey hesitated.

"Tell me," Sangre said firmly. "I seriously doubt you can anything to shock me, not after what has already transpired...and what I used to do."

"Ruthven...did something..." Aubrey said slowly. "He drank my blood...and then, I think, gave it to Gille. I don't know, it was very strange."

Sangre went still. "What?" he asked softly. "Are you certain?"

"As certain as I can be," Aubrey said, scowling at the desktop. He glanced up at his father, who had a strange look on his face. It was part disbelief, part suspicion...and Aubrey swore he almost looked excited.

Standing, Sangre began to rifle through his books in earnest, setting several aside after flipping through them, all but tossing some aside in his impatience. "Are you positive that is what happened, Brey?" Sangre demanded.

"I don't know," Aubrey snapped. "I said it was all very strange, and he fed from me three different times. To the best of my knowledge, yes, that is what happened. Who can say for certain though? I was half asleep and scared at the time." He covered his face with his hand for a moment. "There was blood everywhere."

"Hmm," Sangre said absently, then gave a soft "Ah ha!" and sat back down again. "Here we are - medical treatises on vampires. Most of them are concerning the blood fixation – that a vampire can only feed from the human from whom he first takes blood." He opened the book and gave it to Aubrey. "The accepted theory is that despite bonds of family, each person's blood is in some way wholly unique. This was one argument for never freeing Pets – they could not survive without their masters, and so would be slaves anyway."

Aubrey frowned as he read, eyes snapping open wide as he comprehended the words. "This...proposes that's not true." He looked up at his father. "What in the hell are you doing with so many illegal books."

Sangre snorted in amusement. "Jealous?"

Glaring, Aubrey looked back down at the book. "This says that there are different kinds of blood, but not as unique as we currently believe..."

"Yes," Sangre said. "Vampires can only feed on the blood of their masters. If they tried to feed off someone else, it would not suffice. They would starve. This would indicate that no two people have exactly the same kind of blood...yet Ruthven used your blood to save Gille."

Aubrey frowned in thought. "Maybe it's only a difference that affects vampires, not humans."

"That could be," Sangre agreed. "Most of us did not believe it, though. If it were true, the vampires would not have thrived as they did for so long, before they agreed to being enslaved."

"What!" Aubrey dropped the book he was holding. "What in the hell do you mean 'agreed to being enslaved'?"

Sangre quirked a brow. "The situation is far more complicated than you can possibly imagine, Brey."

"Not for lack of trying," Aubrey snapped. "You're the one who won't let me get involved."

"For your own good," Sangre said, voice taking on a heat of its own. "The people who killed your mother will not hesitate to kill you too! That should be obvious."

"So what?" Aubrey snarled. "Everything comes at a risk."

He started to say more, but the shadows which appeared in his father's eyes stopped him short.

"And what," Sangre said quietly, "would you do if one day they killed your sister, instead of you? That is what they did to me. I ignored their threats, determined to take them on -- and instead they killed your mother and Mina. Is that what you want, Brey? Let the past lie."

Biting back an angry curse, Aubrey bent to pick up the dropped book. Silence fell for several minutes, until at last he forced himself to stir. "What was all that nonsense about vampires choosing enslavement?"

"Oh, how long ago is it now? Well over a hundred years. Must be closer to a hundred and fifty now..." Sangre sighed. "It is buried knowledge, like so much else where the vampires are concerned. They were created by mistake, though I could never learn anything more than that." He glared at his books; clearly this was a sore point. "Anyway, they got out of control, or so it's said. It was decided by everyone, including the leader of the vampires - the Prince, they called him -- that it would be best if his race was annihilated. If they continued to grow in power and numbers, they would eventually destroy the human race."

Aubrey frowned. "That seems cruel."

"Yes," Sangre said. "There were many vampires who disagreed, obviously, with their Prince. One week before the agreement was to be signed, the Prince died. It was, naturally, an accident. No one believed it for a moment, but no one could ever figure out who actually did it. So an accident it remains. Someone else stepped into his place, and agreed to his people's enslavement rather than their demise."

"How...how do you know all this?"

Sangre smiled sadly. "Because once I believed very strongly in freeing them, and took a great many risks to learn all I possibly good. Many secrets cost me gold, others cost me favors...and some cost me blood. In the end, I paid a price I could not bear." He toyed with the wedding ring he still wore, turning it round and round, the heavy ruby set in it glinting in the fire light. "When I found you, Brey,' he said, not looking up, "you were covered in blood. You did not stop crying for nearly a week. It was much longer before you stopped calling for your mother and Mina."

Aubrey looked down at his own hands, not certain what to say. His father had never volunteered such information before, and he was at a loss as to what to do with it.

A servant knocked on the door, announcing the arrival of the requested tea.

Sangre coughed, and Aubrey stood to fetch the tea and pour for both of them. When they were both settled again, Sangre spoke. "The authorities came while you were all asleep, and spoke with Stregoni and I. They are presently scouring the countryside for William, and have issued alerts to other villages. One way or another, we will find the bastard."

"What will we do with him?" Aubrey said, his imagination supplying plenty of satisfying methods of revenge.

"That will be determined after we catch him, and all affected parties are able to decide," Sangre replied, the tone of his voice implying that his own imagination was just as satisfying.

Aubrey took a sip of his tea, dark and sweet, staring at it a moment before finally speaking again. "Stregoni said Carmilla has taken a turn for the worse."

"Yes," Sangre said, face turning dark and stony. "If she does not recover in the next few days...I..." He trailed off, staring at his own tea, looking troubled.

Aubrey did not press him to finish.

He struggled to think of something else to say, mouth quirking as something indeed came to him. "Stregoni said you are keeping the Blackfields hostage."

"Yes," Sangre said, his own mouth quirking, and for a moment father and son looked very much alike. "I would go and fetch their son, but in light of what I learned from Gille, I feel perhaps the lad is doing better without their overzealous fretting. Stregoni will likely go see to the boy once everyone here is doing better."

"You mean once Gille is awake," Aubrey muttered, then realized he'd spoken the thought aloud.

His father only laughed however. "Noticed that too, eh? I tried to speak to Gille about it, but he will not discuss it. If there was one trait I wish my brother and I had not passed on as well as we did, it would be the obstinacy.

Aubrey snorted, unable to argue that one. There was no denying that they all of them were a trifle to stubborn, from his father to Carmilla to himself and right on to Gille. "Is your brother obstinate, too, then?"

"Yes," Sangre said. "Far more than me, even." He frowned, then shook his head. "We have enough problems, without discussing my idiot brother."

"You know, he's the only one you talk about less than mother."

Sangre looked up, every line of age showing in his face now. "We neither of us could handle losing the women we love. I have dealt with it better than him, but not by much. Gille would not want it discussed, for he is ferociously guarded about such things, but if I had not taken him from his father I have no doubt he would be dead. There is..an arrangement, I guess you might say. I raise Gille, he leaves all of us alone."

Aubrey nodded, feeling more tired than ever. Secrets and secrets -- how much more of his life and family had never been told to him? Why was he so damnably ignorant?"

"This is the second time your Pet has gone to sleep like this," Sangre said suddenly. "Why did he do it the first time?"

"I don't know," Aubrey said. "Though, uh, there were things about that night I never told, that I guess I should tell now."

Sangre's brows went up. "Do tell."

Wincing, Aubrey told him all that had actually transpired.

When he finished, Sangre leaned back in his chair, arms folded across his chest, and simply sat thinking for several long moments.

Aubrey sat nervously, wondering if they were about to get into another shouting match -- and realized he'd rather enjoyed that so far there had been no voice raising at all. Not even a moderate loss of temper.

He and his father were getting along. How strange.

"Your vampire," Sangre said at last, "is the strangest thing I've ever heard about. Nothing I've ever read would account for such behavior. He sounds more like the stuff of myth and legend, all of it utter rot and nonsense."

Aubrey grimaced. "I guess that's what we get for letting Gille do the shopping."

"I'll be certain to take him to task for it," Sangre said, smiling.

Before he could catch himself, Aubrey smiled back.

Aspen

(chapter thirteen)

Stregoni was used to being woken in all sorts of ways – screams, pounding upon his door, his mother shaking him hard. Every crude way of waking a person had been inflicted upon him for as long as he could remember.

What he couldn't remember was being woken gently. The closest he got was waking up groggily on his own, usually to the clatter and racket of the houses around him as people prepared for their days, and servants ran about doing the earliest chores.

Usually, he was slow to wake, despite – or maybe because of – the rough ways in which he was always woken. His parents were much better about it, Stregoni envied them.

Today, however, he was immediately wide awake.

It took him several minutes to figure out that's what was so strange. He was completely alert. Not even remotely groggy.

What had woken him?

Not the sunlight, though that was enough to make him feel horrendously guilty – he was always up with the sun, if not well before. He could not remember the last time he had slept in so late, minus those occasions where he was still awake when the sun rose.

The location? He realized he was still in Gille's room – on Gille's bed, because Aubrey had put him there and he'd been too tired to leave it again once Aubrey vanished. That was certainly enough to rattle him awake...but that wasn't what actually woke him.

Stregoni sat up slowly, absently lifting a hand to his cheek – and then it suddenly struck him why he'd woken

Someone had touched him, or it had seemed like someone had touched him. Softly, like a caress.

He turned slowly toward Gille, wondering if he was about to be shoved from the bed, or taunted, or simply ignored.

Nothing of the kind, it seemed. Gille was still fast asleep.

Stregoni touched his own cheek again, frowning in thought. Had he dreamed it? He would have sworn...but that was not Gille's style, and anyway he had no reason to touch. Gille was in no condition to do those things that were the only reason he ever touched Stregoni.

A dream, then. A phantom touch he'd wanted badly enough to be real, he'd forced himself awake.

Idiot.

Sighing, Stregoni shoved back the chaotic mess that his hair had become and reached out to feel Gille's pulse, check the bruise and faint scars that were all that remained of the wound that should have been fatal.

Gille's skin was still paler than it should be, but he'd gain his full color in another day or so. His skin was warm to the touch, but not feverish. Soft, he could not help but notice. Gille always had such soft skin.

A knock on the door made him jump, and flinch guiltily back. Scrambling off the bed, he left the bedroom, crossed the sitting room, and opened the door to reveal a servant bearing a heavy tray. "Doctor, I hope I didn't wake you."

"No," Stregoni said. "Who ordered that?"

"Lord Aubrey said I should take up breakfast and see if anyone was awake yet. He said you likely would be, Doctor. Shall I set it on that table?"

"Um—yes. Thank you." Stregoni moved out of the way, standing quietly until the servant was done fussing with the tray, then absently thanked him before he was left once more alone.

He moved numbly to the table, realizing for the first time that Brey – and likely everyone now – knew about his feelings for Gille.

Gille would probably not take to it well – or perhaps he'd be vastly amused. It would certainly be just one more way to mock him for it. Stregoni winced and moved to the table, slumping down in a chair and preparing his tea with no enthusiasm. His stomach was far too knotted for food to appeal.

The idea of going back to bed was tempting, but that just made him think about the fact he'd just spent the entire night in Gille's bed, next to Gille, and he was just grateful that he'd woken up first. He shuddered to think what might have happened otherwise.

Without even realizing it, his hand strayed once more to his cheek, and he stared miserably at his tea before finally attempting a sip.

He set it aside immediately, suspicions confirmed. He was simply too nervous and unsettled to eat.

What was everyone else up to? He should go check on Carmilla, and if the weather was improved, he should go check on Tony. The poor thing probably hated having his parents gone for so long, even if it was the best medicine.

Sighing, he rubbed his temples, willing himself not to get a headache on top of the knots in his stomach.

Dropping his hands, he picked his tea up again and forced himself to take another sip, and then another. If he could get down a full cup of tea, he stood a chance at eating a proper breakfast. He would need it, whether he wanted it or not – his day was going to be a long one.

He had just started to eat when he heard movement from the bedroom, and only then realized he was making himself far too cozy in Gille's room, eating breakfast like he belonged there.

Ignoring the ache that thought left in his chest, Stregoni pushed his food away and made his way to the bedroom. "What are you doing up?" He demanded, the doctor and the lover in him both furious. "Get back in that damned bed."

Gille paused where he was slowly and laboriously going through his wardrobe. "I'm fine," he said, then went back to pulling out clothes.

"Like hell you're fine!" Stregoni snapped, stomping across the room to grab Gille's arm, pulling him away from the wardrobe. "You're a bloody idiot, that's what you are. Get back in bed this instant or I'll put you there!"

"Oh?" Gille asked softly, looking entirely too smug and amused for a man who was obviously weak and tired and straining himself. "Do, please."

Stregoni glared. "Bastard," he hissed. "You will not undo all the work that was done to save your inconsiderate, ungrateful, ass. Get. Back. In. Bed. I am the medical expert present, and I say you are not fit to leave your bed. Get back in it!"

Gille laughed. "No."

"Damn it, Gille, that was not a request. It was an order."

"I cannot," Gille replied, pulling off his shirt and slowly pulling on another. He was far too pale, and a fine sheen of sweat covered his brow. His hair was a mess, tumbling about everywhere.

Stregoni balled his hands into fists to avoid reaching out to smooth the messy strands back. "Why not?" he demanded.

"I have an appointment," Gille said shortly. "It will not keep."

"With whom?" Stregoni said. "I think they will understand if you say that you cannot make it for fear of almost getting yourself killed a second time."

Gille did not bother to look at him as he fought with his breeches. Stregoni glared, too worried and furious to be distracted. When he was finally dressed, Gille finally looked up again. "My appointments are none of your business," he said coldly. "I thank you for tending me, Doctor. I am quite well."

"Like hell!" Stregoni bellowed. "Get back in bed!"

Instead, Gille stalked toward him.

"Get away from me," Stregoni snarled, but he'd barely gotten the words out when Gille's hands landed heavily on his shoulders, and dragged him forward, crushing him against Gille's chest.

Then Gille was kissing him, deep and hard and long, and for a moment Stregoni lost track of his thoughts.

They returned full force, however, when he saw up close just how not well Gille really was.

"You need to rest," he whispered.

"It's none of your business," Gille said, voice as cold as the snow outside. "I'll thank you to stop mother-henning me. I outgrew a nanny years ago." He pushed Stregoni away, and strode to the door.

Stregoni saw red. Not even truly realizing what he did, he reached out and grabbed the nearest object -- a heavy dark blue vase filled with Syrian Mallow. It shattered against the door, just ahead of Gille, startling him into stillness.

Gille whipped around, eyes filled with fury, and Stregoni let him have it.

"I thought you were dead," he bellowed. "You were bleeding too heavily, there was already too much blood lost, and if not for Ruthven you would be dead, you selfish, ungrateful ass. All I've done is worry about you, all you do is manipulate me—and it's none of my business?" He grabbed something else to throw, not even certain what it was, and kept throwing and shouting until suddenly Gille was in front of him, and kissing him again, and Stregoni wanted to struggle and beat the bastard senseless—but Gille was not yet fit, and he could not forget that.

"Stay out of it, Carrot," Gille whispered, their mouths not quite touching.

Then he was gone, and Stregoni was left alone. Again. Confused and miserable. Again.

"Damn it," he said, and buried his face in his hands, sinking to sit on the floor. "Why can't I hate you?"

What in the hell did 'stay out of it' mean? Was that supposed to make sense? Stay out of what? Gille's business? Gille's life?

He reached up to touch his cheek again, remembering the soft caress from his dream.

Standing up, he brushed his clothes off and then strode through the mess he'd made to the door, kicking away a shard of porcelain.

What had he really expected? For Gille to have...had a change of heart because he'd nearly died?

That would imply Gille had a heart, and Stregoni was beginning to seriously doubt that.

If only he could give up on Gille, but he sensed he'd sooner give up practicing medicine.

"Good," Stregoni murmured, as she stopped before Tony's door and bobbed a curtsy.

Letting himself inside, Stregoni strode across the room to the bed, where another maid sat beside the bed, a closed book in her lap. Tony slept peacefully, but he could see at a glance it was not as deep and still a sleep as that which afflicted Ruthven and Carmilla. "How is he?"

"Much better since his lordship came and kicked up that fuss," the maid said. "He scared the Blackfield's good and proper, put the shame to them, put that quack in his place, eh?"

Stregoni paused in checking Tony over, confused. "His lordship? Lord Sangre came out this way?"

"Eh? No, Doctor. I meant the other one – his nephew, isn't it? Begging your pardon for any rudeness. His lordship showed up icy as you please, had them shaking in their slippers right off." She smiled blandly. "Not that we would be eavesdropping on the conversations of our betters, now."

"Of course," Stregoni said, equally bland.

She smiled. "As I was saying, the downstairs maids were cleaning at the time, supervised by the head footman like, and they heard the whole thing – accidentally, like. His lordship summoned William, and proceeded to question him on all sorts of medical things. No idea his lordship was so educated, but then again he made it clear you were a close and very dear friend of the family. I expect he picked up the wisdom from you, Doctor."

"Indeed," Stregoni said.

"Anyway, he asked question after question, and that no account quack couldn't answer. Was humiliated right good and proper, he was, all in front of the master and mistress. Then his lordship turned on them, and had them shaking like leaves for daring to hurt you and all. When he was finished, he offered them a chance to make reparations to you, Doctor. Did they?"

Stregoni nodded absently. "Are you quite certain it was Gille who was here?"

The maid laughed softly. "Oh, yes, Doctor. Beggin your pardon for any forwardness, but we'd all know that one on sight. Pretty as anything, his lordship. Long brown hair, the green eyes as delicate as porcelain." She sighed softly, hands clasped in her lap. "Aye, it was him, sure enough."

Sure enough, Stregoni thought faintly. What in the world? Why would Gille go to so much trouble...

No wonder William had been so furious with him – why he had poisoned the Pets, or attempted to. Stregoni had long been the target of Gille's ability to find the weakest spot and go for the kill. He could not imagine that William, weak and so obviously a charlatan, would have endured it for long.

"Are the master and mistress returning?" the maid asked.

"Eventually," Stregoni said. "Not any time soon, I should think."

The maid nodded. "Good. Begging your pardon, Doctor, for any impertinence. They're good, kind people, more often than not – but kindness can kill, eh?'

"Yes," Stregoni replied. "Kindness can kill. I have brought some teas and tincture that I think will help him, though I can see you all have done quite well on your own. Keep it up, and if he takes a turn, send for me at Lord Sangre's home."

He looked out the window, to see that night had fallen well and truly. Too late, then, to attempt any sort of travel. "I will have to leave in the morning. I do not suppose there is a bed I might steal for the night?"

"Of course, Doctor," the maid said, and stood up. Briskly she made certain Tony was comfortable, taking up the tins and bottles which Stregoni had set out, then led him from the room and down the hall to a room. "We'll have dinner sent up straight away. Anything else you would like, Doctor?"

Stregoni shook his head, and set his things down, suddenly extremely tired. "No, I thank you. Food would be greatly appreciated."

The maid bobbed a curtsy, and closed the door quietly behind her.

Moving to the bed, Stregoni flopped down on it, and fell almost instantly asleep, too tired even to dwell on Gille's strange behavior.

Globe Amaranth

(chapter fourteen)

Aubrey opened his eyes slowly, still more asleep than awake–then he realized what he was lying against was not a pillow, and his eyes snapped open. He sat up jerkily, and saw that sometime in the night, he'd moved to rest against Ruthven.

Grimacing at himself, he shoved back the blankets and climbed out of bed. Strolling into the sitting room, he glanced at the clock and saw it was well past ten in the morning.

Being home was making him lazy.

Eschewing a bath for the moment, he freshened up at the pitcher in his bedroom, then changed into clean clothes. Slipping on a pair of buckled shoes, he strode to the bed to give Ruthven one last look over, reaching out despite himself to comb lightly through the beeswax-colored hair.

If Ruthven felt the touch, he gave no sign of it.

Sighing softly, Aubrey finally turned away to see what he might do today.

Downstairs, he knocked upon the door of his father's study, but heard no reply from within. Opening the door, he found it was empty.

Frowning in thought, he closed the door and headed for the breakfast room. Three sides of it were glass from ceiling to about halfway down the wall. There was a fireplace in the fourth wall, the door in the corner. Normally it was a cheerful room in which to begin the day, but with the curtains pulled back to reveal the endlessly falling white, the overall impression was one of weary resignation.

The room was empty, so Aubrey left to look elsewhere.

Spying a maid dusting in a hallway, he asked her where his father might be found.

"With her ladyship, my lord," the maid replied.

"Thank you," Aubrey said, ignoring the way she turned bright red while speaking to him.

Making his way back upstairs, he headed for his sister's room.

Sure enough, there was his father, sitting in an armchair he had pulled over to the bedside.

He did not look up as Aubrey approached, and Aubrey wondered if his arrival had even been noticed.

Drawing close to the chair, his eyes were caught by movement, and he looked down to see—

"*You* drew the picture in my study?" he blurted out, too shocked by what he was seeing to remain silent.

Sangre's head whipped up and around, hand stopping mid-stroke in the middle of the portrait he was drawing of a sleeping Carmilla. Aubrey knew the art style – it was indeed the same as the portrait of his mother and Mina. The same as the sketches he and Ruthven had found in his mother's room.

"We always thought it was mother or Mina who drew..."

"Brey," Sangre greeted, looking back down at the sketch. "I did not hear you come in. You look well rested."

"Yes," Aubrey said. "Why did you never say you were the artist in the family?"

Sangre gave a minute shrug. "Because I lost all interest after they died, and it made Carmilla happy to think she acquired her talent from her mother..." His face tightened briefly. "Of late, the desire to draw appears to have returned. I thought to sketch while I watched over her..."

Aubrey nodded, still unable to believe it – his stern, strict, reserved father was responsible for all the beautiful artwork, the portrait he'd always kept. He looked at Carmilla. "How is she?"

"No better," Sangre said heavily. "I fear..." He shook his head. "I hope she at least wakes up soon, for the measure I must take will require her knowledge and approval."

"What are you talking about?" Aubrey asked.

Sangre only shook his head. "I must speak with your sister first."

Recognizing the finality of his tone, Aubrey reluctantly dropped the matter.

Normally, he would have argued and pushed. Now...as strange as it still was, to be getting along with his father, it was far from being an unpleasant strangeness. He was reluctant to start arguing again. "Has Stregoni returned yet?" he asked instead.

"No," Sangre replied, and resumed sketching again. "I do not imagine he or Gille will return for another day or two."

"Gille?" Aubrey asked. "I did not know Gille had left. Why in the hell would he? Surely he is still recovering, and this weather would only acerbate the problem. What the devil is he thinking?"

Sangre sighed. "He went to see his father. Though I tried, I could not persuade him from going."

Aubrey frowned. "I guess I never really bothered to understand the entire situation with Gille. Why does he live with us, rather than with his own father?"

"Because my fool brother is no longer fit to be a parent," Sangre said sharply, and drew a line in the portrait with a tad more force than was necessary. "As I said before, we both lost the women that were the center of our world. I learned to live without them, though I hate it. I chose to live for them, and for our children. My brother..." Sangre sighed. "My brother chose to hate his child."

"I admit Gille is more than a little difficult to get along with, but...well, to be fair, I'm certain people say the same about me as often as not. Why would his own father hate him, though?"

Sangre shook his head. "I promised Gille I would not discuss his problems, and I have already said too much. To be honest, I do not even know the whole of it myself. Suffice to say my brother was always a fool, and has only grown worse over the years. Gille will not cut him away entirely, though I keep trying to persuade him to do exactly that. Perhaps his little doctor will have more luck."

"Stregoni?" Aubrey said. "Until recently, I always thought those two hated each other. I'm still confused as to what exactly is going on between them, though Stregoni's feelings are plain enough."

"I doubt either of them knows what is between them, as complicated as they have made the situation," Sangre said with a snort. "Hopefully they will work it out before it's too late." He shook his head. "Young people."

Aubrey copied the derisive snort. "This from a man who was apparently in quite the scandalous relationship when he was young." He moved to sit on the edge of Carmilla's bed, reaching out idly to stroke his sister's hand, hating that she was so still. "Did anyone else know about it? I cannot imagine your parents would have approved."

"A few very close friends knew," Sangre said, setting aside the drawing of Carmilla, and beginning something new. Aubrey could not see what from his new position on the bed. "My parents knew, or suspected, I think, but chalked it up to a boy sowing his wild oats." He looked up to glance at Aubrey, then Carmilla, and smiled ever so faintly, briefly, before returning his gaze to his sketch. "Her guardian did not care what Carmilla did, so long as she married well and was discreet about anything untoward. Rumors did begin to circulate, of course, for your mother and Mina were both beautiful." He shook his head, smirking briefly. "More than a few men made impolite inquiries, I think out of jealousy more than anything.

"I always thought you were so proper," Aubrey said, shaking his head and laughing.

Sangre looked at him in amusement. "Children never think their parents capable of being normal people, not until they are much older, if ever." He returned to his sketch, and it was so bizarre to see his father doing such a thing. Aubrey could only stare in wonder. "The increase of those rumors was one of the reasons we moved out here after we were married. Until then, this manor had been closed for years. It was hard, adjusting to country life, but we found ourselves fond of it rather quickly."

Aubrey nodded. He wasn't certain he'd ever get used to the idea that the father he'd thought he'd always known had in fact been more than a bit of a rebel, and one with two lovers.

A sudden thought occurred to him. "What did your brother think of all this?"

"He did not care," Sangre said. "We are twins, but we were never particularly close. It was better, after he got married. His wife brought out the better parts of him which he had never bothered to display before. He thought I was a fool, but I thought the same of him. Once his wife died, he became despicable." Sangre's mouth tightened with anger. "I will never forget the way Gille looked the day I finally brought him home."

Aubrey frowned, but did not ask. "Why does Gille still go to see him, then?"

"That is complicated," Sangre replied.

"Everything is complicated," Aubrey muttered, turning to look at his sister again.

Sangre sighed. "Yes, it is." He set aside his newest sketch, and began still another.

Aubrey looked in surprise at the new one – it was of him, sitting on Carmilla's bed. He coughed and looked away, reaching out restlessly to stroke his sister's hair.

"I take it your vampire has not stirred," Sangre said into the silence.

"No," Aubrey replied. "He was still fast asleep when I woke this morning."

Sangre looked up. "You should go eat something, Brey. I cannot imagine you bothered before finding me here. Go and eat. The inspector said that, weather permitting, he could stop by today to give us a progress report on the hunt for William."

"Have you eaten?" Aubrey asked suspiciously.

"Yes," Sangre said. "Go do likewise."

Unable to think of a good reason to protest, Aubrey accepted the dismissal.

Instead of going downstairs, he made his way slowly back to his own room, mind spinning with dozens upon dozens of thoughts. His father, his sister, Gille and Stregoni, Ruthven...

He was so lost in thought, he barely avoided running smack into the footman carrying a large bathtub into his room.

"What is going on here?" he asked, following them inside, watching as they set it in place, and still more footmen began to appear with hot water. "I did not call for a bath."

"I did."

Aubrey whipped around and stared. "You're awake."

Ruthven smiled from where he leaned lazily in the doorway between bedroom and sitting room. "Master, it is good to see you are looking well."

"Damn it, Ruthven!" Aubrey said, annoyed though he could not say why, exactly. "Why did you not come and tell me you were awake?"

He realized too late he should not have gotten close, for the moment he was within reach, Ruthven snagged him close and took his mouth in a searing kiss.

"Good morning, master," Ruthven murmured when he finally allowed the kiss to end. His fingers trailed lightly over Aubrey's throat. "Are you sufficiently recovered in strength to feed me?"

Aubrey realized suddenly the servants were still going in and out of the room to fill the bath, and felt his face go warm. "Could we discuss this in the bedroom, please?"

A glint sparked in Ruthven's eyes. "If you insist, master," he said, looking pleased.

"That is not what I meant," Aubrey hissed. "You are not getting away with *that* again."

"Yes, master," Ruthven said.

Aubrey didn't believe him for a second. Pushing Ruthven away, he preceded him into the bedroom, moving to the window to look out at the damnable snow. It was everywhere. Only the trees were at all identifiable, and they seemed to be rapidly losing the battle to winter.

Warm lips touched his throat, gentle against the mostly faded but still present bruise.

"Why do you keep feeding from my throat?" he asked. "It's entirely improper." The better question, perhaps, was why he kept permitting it.

He pointedly ignored all the heated answers his body was supplying, and attempted to pull free, but Ruthven was pressed full against his backside, one arm braced on the glass, the other wrapped around his waist. Aubrey was rather efficiently trapped, though he sensed he would be set free if he really insisted.

Which begged the question why he was not insisting, but he stubbornly ignored the question so to avoid having to supply the answer.

Teeth nipped lightly at his skin, making him gasp and jerk.

"Stop it," he said. "It really is unseemly."

"Mmm," Ruthven murmured, tongue lapping to soothe the sting from his nips. "You look good with it, master. You were made to bear the marks of a vampire's embrace."

"A what—" Aubrey gasped as Ruthven chose that moment to bite, jerking at the sudden pain – but then he felt suddenly lethargic, as though he had heavily imbibed and would shortly fall asleep. He stilled in Ruthven's arms, unprotesting as he was bundled close, his head tipped to the side to give Ruthven better access.

Somewhere in there, it had stopped hurting as badly.

When Ruthven stopped feeding, the world spun, until Aubrey realized he was lying on the bed. He stared up at the canopy, trying to figure out what exactly had transpired.

Ruthven appeared over him, and now he felt the vampire's weight and warmth. He was still too mellow to protest though, and could not even muster the energy to push Ruthven away when he bent to steal a kiss. Instead, he gave in to it, clinging for dear life as Ruthven plundered his mouth. He tasted like blood, but was also hot and spicy and male.

Aubrey realized that somewhere in the past several days, he had grown entirely too used to Ruthven's kisses. He feared he was beginning to need them. "What—" he was cut off as Ruthven's hands began to take liberties, and realized suddenly his own hands were taking some liberties of their own.

Damn it, he'd not intended his to happen.

Yet he could not muster a protest when Ruthven pulled him up just enough to discard his shirt entirely.

"What was it you said a moment ago?" he asked, managing to get the words out one by one between kisses and caresses. This was nothing like the last time, which had been fast and feverish. This was just as heated and consuming, but slower. Almost...sweeter.

Ruthven kissed him again, thorough and lingering. "You were made to wear the mark's of a vampire's embrace."

Aubrey groaned as that statement was followed by another kiss, this one faster and hotter, accompanied by Ruthven's hand cupping his cock through his breeches. "What...what does that mean?" He reached up to shove back Ruthven's shirt, one hand trailing down the fine, smooth chest, the other going up to touch the velvet collar wrapped around Ruthven's neck.

Catching his hand, Ruthven kissed the palm, then his wrist. "These days, nothing." His eyes, still so dark and strange, almost seemed to glow. "Once, a very long time ago, it was considered an honor to be strong enough to be fed upon so voraciously."

"You know so much," Aubrey said, freeing his capture hand to reach up with both to lightly touch Ruthven's face. "What are you?"

"Only your Pet," Ruthven replied, hands going still as they stared at each other.

Aubrey shook his head slightly, never breaking contact. "You are more than that."

"No," Ruthven said softly. "I am yours, and nothing more."

He could only continue to stare, captured by the strange, beautiful eyes, and the wealth of emotions he could see now, simmering there just below the surface. "What color are your eyes?" he said, realizing suddenly he was whispering.

"All colors," Ruthven said simply. "And none." He turned his head to kiss the palm of Aubrey's hand again.

Though there any number of reasons to succumb to this was a bad idea, Aubrey could suddenly recall none of them. Grasping Ruthven's shoulders, he dragged him down for another kiss, and gave himself up to Ruthven's wants.

Carrot Flower

(chapter fifteen)

It was the cold which finally forced his hand.

He was not thrilled to be here, even as some traitorous part of him could not help but thrill at any chance to see Gille.

That he was the world's biggest idiot was painfully obvious, but if that's the way it was, that's the way it was, and there was nothing to do about it but make do.

Making certain his horse was comfortably settled, he finally abandoned the meager warmth of the stable and trekked toward the house.

He raised a hand toward the knocker, then hesitated. Lord Sangre had told him to check on Gille – had, in fact, seemed worried about him. If he knocked, he stood a chance of being locked out. Assuming he wasn't already, but...

Stregoni tried to the door, expecting to meet with resistance, but it gave easily under his hand. Swallowing, wondering what in the hell he was doing and how much trouble this would earn him, he pushed the door opened and slipped inside.

The house was warm, at least compared to the outside. He shucked his wet outdoor clothes and set his bag close to them. Shivering, he looked around.

Dust was the dominant smell. It was obvious that the house received only the most basic of cleaning, and even that seemed half-hearted at best. The few doors he could see where firmly shut, heavy layers of dust coating the handles – he would be willing to bet they were seldom, if ever, used.

Nearby he could see the room into which Gille had locked him. It alone did not match the disuse of the others.

All right. Now that he was here, what was he supposed to do? Find Gille before someone else noticed the stranger skulking about and tossed him out on his ear as a thief or something, but what would he did if – when – he found Gille?

Wondering what the hell was wrong with him, in no mood to supply the obvious answer, Stregoni opted to try the stairs.

He wandered back and forth down a handful of hallways before he at last came to a door which was just barely ajar, and from which spilled warm orange-yellow light. Hoping it contained what he sought, Stregoni headed toward it and gently pushed the door open.

Gille was stretched out on a chaise lounge which had been moved to set right in front of a roaring fire. The room was almost stifling. He realized after a moment that Gille was asleep. Relieved for the moment, because he was in no hurry for the inevitable arguments and anger and confusion, he crossed the carpeted room slowly and perched on the very edge of the backless chaise.

His eyes widened as he got a good look at Gille, hidden until then by the long, loose fall of his beautiful hair.

It looked as though he'd been the one to receive a punch or two, this time. One eye was swollen rather badly, and his bottom was lip split near the corner of his mouth, which also showed signs of swelling. Stregoni reached out to lightly touch them, frowning in concern. Had his father done this? Why would he strike his own son in such fashion? Had it been someone else?

Gille's eyes fluttered open at the gentle touch, but Stregoni could see from his eyes that he was barely awake, if at all. "Carrot..."

Stregoni said nothing, merely gently pushed back Gille's unlaced shirt to see where else he might be hurt, but his questing fingers found nothing but smooth, unmarred skin.

"Dreaming..." Gille said softly, the words barely audible.

Suddenly Stregoni noticed something he had missed before, too obsessed with Gille and the harm done him. Laudanum—he definitely smelled traces of laudanum. Had Gille drugged himself to sleep? That wasn't like Gille at all. Gille hated medicine, especially the more potent ones.

He looked up at the soft touch of fingers to his cheek, shivering as he realized the way Gille caressed him was the touch he remembered from his dream. Shocked, he stared at Gille, whom he could now see was definitely dosed on laudanum. "Gille..." He shook his head, not certain what else to say.

"Should not be here," Gille said, the words coming slowly, as though each weighed heavily and was ponderous to speak.

Fingers landed heavily on the back of Stregoni's neck, but despite the slight clumsiness of the gesture he found himself tugged forward, splaying his hands on Gille's chest for balance as Gille's mouth landed awkwardly on his. He tasted of laudanum and brandy, a hint of clove.

It was nothing like the hard, sure, bewitching kisses with which Gille had taunted him time and again. No, this one was clumsy and drugged and slow – but struck him to the core all the same, for there was a...genuineness to it that left him reeling.

The taste of blood was what finally made him pull away, and he reached out to gently touch the split in Gille's lip, frowning in concern. "You need help," he said, wondering if this had happened because Gille had already been too sick and weak when he'd left Sangre Manor.

A hand wrapped around his wrist with surprising strength, keeping him in place. "Stay," Gille said softly, before his eyes drifted shut again.

Sighing softly, Stregoni shifted to try and settle more comfortably, wishing he could simply stretch out with Gille on the chaise. He feared, however, what would happen when the effects of the laudanum finally wore off. Would the Gille with which he was far more familiar return? Shove him off and begin to mock him?

The thought was a painful one, and Stregoni looked over this softer Gille, wondering what it meant – if anything. That familiar caress, that slow, sweet kiss, the way Gille had asked him to stay.

Eventually the fingers around his wrist relaxed enough he could withdraw it, but even then he could not make himself move away. Instead he reached out to card a hand through Gille's hair, smoothing out the tangles as best he could, admiring the softness and the way it shone in the firelight.

Sometime later, when the fire had dimmed a bit, Gille's eyes opened again. They were still drugged, but not quite as heavily. "Carrot."

Stregoni said nothing, afraid that speaking would wake them both from this strange dream. He liked this Gille, though he hated that laudanum was needed to induce it. An arm slid around his waist, a heavy, solid weight, Gille's hand sliding up his spine to push Stregoni down, bring him close again.

He buried his fingers in Gille's hair, cradling his head, more than happy to lose himself in another of those slow burning kisses, feeling it all the way to his bones.

The slamming of the door against the wall as it was thrown open made him jerk, teeth accidentally grazing Gille's lip. He sat up and stared, disoriented for a moment as he wondered why Lord Sangre was here and looking so terrible.

Then he realized this wasn't Sangre, but his brother – George Bathory. Gille's father.

He was unkempt, a rough beard covering much of his face, wearing clothes that should have been replaced a long time ago.

Stregoni realized he was also furious.

Next to him, Gille suddenly swore – and he could hear that Gille was now entirely lucid.

"Damn it, Carrot," Gille said, but the rest of what he was going to say never got spoken, as he abruptly shoved Stregoni away and stood up, tugging his shirt back into place even as his father grabbed him.

"Well, well," George said, and Stregoni had never heard a voice so full of hate and rage. "Seems my selfish, backstabbing, murderous son has been keeping secrets from me. I might have known."

"No, father. I—" Gille's words were lost in a cry of pain as he was punched hard in the stomach, then cast aside.

"Stregoni," Gille gasped out, struggling to get back to his feet. "Run."

Stregoni didn't reply, but he had not intention of leaving when Gille was obviously being abused. He glared as George turned to him, refusing to back down, wondering what in the hell was going on.

"Well, well," George said again. "I recognize that hair – you are the son of that pathetic excuse for a doctor who allowed my son to kill my wife, and made no effort to save her."

What?

Stregoni attempted to stay out of reach, but in the confines of the small room, there was simply no where to go to escape – and he would not leave without Gille.

"No!" Gille said, grabbing his father's arm. "He only came because Uncle told him to, there is nothing—" He let out another cry as George shoved him off, sending him crashing into the wall.

Gille slid slowly down the wall, and did not stir once he slumped on the floor.

Stregoni wondered how the hell Gille knew he'd been sent – then realized suddenly Gille thought he was making it up.

"My brother, I might have known. I don't believe my brother would have sent someone along with explicit orders to kiss you, my son. Obviously, you have listened to nothing I've said." He stalked toward Stregoni, who stumbled away, only to collide with the chaise and go tumbling down upon it.

He was snatched up by the throat, and struggle though he did, George did not appear even to notice. With the firelight behind him, Stregoni could see at a glance that George was heavily drugged on something. What, he did not know.

Gille groaned, and Stregoni could just see from the corner of his eye as Gille slowly stood up again, one hand braced against the wall for support.

"Why were you kissing the good little doctor's son, my child?" George asked in a voice of deceptive softness that made Stregoni truly scared.

"I was dreaming," Gille said, obviously trying for cold and uncaring, but in too much pain to manage it. "It was nothing, father. I always dream strangely when I drink laudanum. You know I love no one but you."

George shook Stregoni hard, and smiled in a way that made Stregoni think of a wolf. "Well, then you will not care if I have a bit of fun with the good little doctor's son."

Stregoni almost corrected him, to say he was a good little doctor now, thanks – but common sense prevailed, and he kept his mouth shut.

He continued to twist and kick and struggle, but if George noticed the pain, he gave no sign of it – and Stregoni had a sneaking suspicion that the man was so heavily doped, he would not notice if someone cut off a limb.

George let him go, but then spun him around and gripped his anew, so that Stregoni was facing the fire – then abruptly grabbed his arm and thrust his hand into the fire.

Stregoni screamed.

Gille screamed louder, and then the whole world dissolved into chaos as father and son struggled, and Stregoni continued to scream and sob for the pain in his hand. His bag, he needed his bag—

Then Gille was on the floor again, whimpering in pain, and Stregoni found himself being held again, barely able to see for the tears of pain streaming from his own eyes.

"Quite the reaction," George said idly, as though discussing a painting. "I think, my child, that you are a liar." He bared his teeth at Stregoni. "Are you and my son in love, good little doctor's son?"

"No," Gille gasped out, face white with pain and, Stregoni realized, fear. "I could never love a worthless, useless doctor. I do not love him."

Stregoni abruptly realized two things.

Gille was lying.

He was not the only one who realized it.

"What did I say, my child, about you loving anyone?" George asked.

Gille, Stregoni realized, looked close to tears. He had never seen Gille so shaken and defeated. He never wanted to see it again.

"That I'm not allowed," Gille said hollowly.

"Why?" George asked, voice silky and lazy, but full of so much menace that Stregoni felt cold.

"Because I killed my mother, and took from you the person you loved, and the woman who loved us both. I do not deserve anyone of my own," Gille said quietly, looking at the carpet as he spoke.

Stregoni stared in shock.

Gille's mother had died in childbirth. That wasn't his fault. It was no one's fault, simply a great tragedy. Did his father really have Gille convinced that he'd murdered his own mother? He'd just been born for fuck's sake.

Was that really what was going on here?

"And what," George continued, "did I say would happen if you were stupid enough to love someone?"

"That you would kill him or her," Gille whispered, then finally looked up. "I do not love him, father. Only you, you know that. Please, stop this. He is not worth all this trouble."

George laughed. "Oh, he is worth it, if only because he is related to that bloody—"

Stregoni took more than a little satisfaction in the way the bastard dropped like a rock, landing amidst the shard of broken porcelain from the vase Stregoni had managed to snatch up while father tormented son.

Grimacing at the pain in his throbbing left hand, he stumbled his way to Gille and helped him up.

"What in the hell did you do?" Gille demanded. "Why the hell are you even here, Carrot. Damn it, I told you to stay out of it!"

"Shut up," Stregoni snapped. "Let's get the hell out of here."

"I can't just leave him," Gille said, fear slipping into his voice. "You don't understand—"

Stregoni blocked him from going toward his unconscious father. "I understand the man is an insane bastard, and that I wish I could kill him the way he was going to kill me," he snarled. "We're going."

"You don't—"

"Damn it, Gille!" Stregoni bellowed. "My hand hurts, you are badly beaten, and I am not leaving here without you, even if that means I must knock you out and drag you home." He reached out with his good hand to grip Gille's shirt, looking up at him pleadingly. "Please."

Gille looked at his father, then at Stregoni, pale eyes full of so much pain. "Carrot...he'll stop at nothing to kill you, now. Unless I convince him not to do it."

"He's demented," Stregoni replied, wishing he could just kill the bastard for being so goddamn cruel to his own son. "You didn't kill your mother, and I'm still alive. I fully intend to stay that way. We're leaving."

"I can't—"

"Do not refuse me!" Stregoni shouted, fisting his hand tightly in the linen of Gille's shirt. Moving without thought, he stepped in close and stood on his toes to mash his mouth against Gille's, tasting blood and laudanum and cloves.

Gille was still a moment, clearly surprised, then slowly began to return the kiss.

Hands landed in his hair, cradling his head gently and then Gille was dominating the kiss, and it was as sweet as the ones Stregoni had stolen earlier, but a thousand times better, because Gille was completely lucid now.

"Gille..."

"Stupid Carrot," Gille whispered. "I told you to stay out of it."

Stregoni just looked at him, caught by the gold-flecked jade eyes. "You were lying, before." He did not bother to clarify what he meant.

Gille was silent at first, emotions flickering ever so briefly across his face. Then he sighed softly, as though he were accepting some terrible defeat. "Yes."

Stregoni wanted to ask a million questions, and beat Gille's foolish, stupid, stubborn head in – but he had not forgotten George, who could wake at any moment. "We're leaving. Do I need to knock you unconscious, or will you come with me?"

"I shouldn't—he'll need to be placated. You don't understand, Carrot."

When had that damned epithet started to sound like an endearment? He wondered now if Gille had always meant it thus.

"Oh, I understand," Stregoni said. "I understand your father is crazy, and I understand it's not your fault your mother died. I understand you deserve love the same as anyone else, and I understand that if we stay here much longer, he probably will kill us – but if we leave, he likely will not. Now, we're leaving."

Gille frowned, but did not protest as Stregoni finally dragged him from the room.

Outside in the hallway, he gently grasped Stregoni's arm, holding up his burned hand for closer examination. "Will it heal?" he asked quietly.

"It'll be fine," Stregoni said. "I have what I need to help it in my bag, downstairs. It's no worse than some of the stuff I managed to do as a child. Come on, we have to hurry."

Getting dressed and to the stable almost proved to be too difficult. Stregoni had never been so tired, or in so much pain. He'd managed a hasty treatment on his hand, but it only dulled the pain, and the hard travelling they'd have to do would not help matters.

He could not bring himself to be bothered by it. He would endure pain a thousand times greater, for the knowledge he now carried.

Gille had said he did not love him – and Gille had been lying, and admitted he'd been lying.

A burned hand, Stregoni decided, was a paltry thing.

And when they returned to Sangre manor, he had a few choice things to explain to Lord Sangre about his contemptuous, pathetic brother.

"Promise you'll return with me to Sangre manor, and stay there," he said.

Gille hesitated.

"I said promise!" Stregoni snarled. "It's the very least you owe me, all things considered."

Gille flinched, but the scathing look he shot Stregoni was so familiar, so Gille, that Stregoni wanted to laugh or cry with relief. "Whatever you say, Carrot."

Deciding it was the best he could expect, Stregoni led the way from the stable, and began the arduous journey home.

Bittersweet Nightshade

(chapter sixteen)

"Oh, my god," Aubrey cried as Stregoni and Gille stumbled in to the library. "What in the hell happened to the two of you?" He scrambled from his seat to help them to the sofa and chairs in one corner. "Your hand, Streg. What in god's name—"

"Brey," Sangre said sharply. "Brandy. Ruthven, ring for tea and food."

Aubrey immediately obeyed, though he was reluctant to leave his friend's side for a moment.

Gille did not look so great either – and wholly unlike himself, sitting quiet and meek on the long sofa. They both looked as though they'd been in a nasty fight, and Stregoni's *hand.*

He brought over the decanter of brandy and two snifters, pouring for both of them. Stregoni downed most of his in one gulp, almost choking – but Gille only shook his head.

"I've had my faculties disrupted more than enough for one day," Gille said. "I'm fine."

Sangre frowned.

Aubrey shrugged and drank the brandy himself. "So what happened to the two of you?"

"Lord George," Stregoni said, tossing back the rest of his brandy and setting the glass aside. "Could you have someone bring my bag to me? I'm afraid I did not have the energy to carry it in myself."

"Of course," Aubrey said, and the moment servants arrived with tea and food, he gave a request that the bag be fetched at once. "Why would Uncle George do this?" he asked, resuming his seat in an armchair near the sofa. Ruthven had decided to perch on the armrest, looking quiet and thoughtful as the rest of them talked. "Father?"

Sangre looked grimly at Gille's injured face, Stregoni's burned hand. "He has gone too far, and I sense he has been going too far for quite some time. I should have ended this matter a long time ago."

"He—" Gille started to speak, then pressed his lips together in a tight line. "I fear he will be coming after us, Uncle. I wanted to stay and placate him—"

"But I talked him out of that stupidity," Stregoni said sharply. He held up his burnt hand. "Lord Sangre, I mean no disrespect, but your brother is quite unstable. He lost his mind when he saw...Gille and I together, and at one point shoved my hand straight into the fire. He did worse besides. I believe he drugged Gille with laudanum, and he was taking something else himself."

Sangre glowered at their injuries. "Saying my brother is 'quite' unstable is a vast understatement. I thought we had him under control." He slid Gille a pensive look. "You did not tell me everything."

Gille said nothing, merely glared at the trays of food on the low table.

"I know you feel guilty, Gille," Sangre said, voice gentler than Aubrey had ever heard it. "Your father is not your fault –

he was never the most stable person to begin with, I have tried to tell you this."

Stregoni lay a hand on Gille's thigh, stilling whatever protest he'd been about to make. Aubrey had never seen his cousin so...compliant. It was the strangest thing.

"Lord Sangre," Stregoni said, "you have no idea what your brother has been doing all these years."

Gille's face tightened. "I would really rather keep my personal business to myself, Carrot," he snarled.

"He tried to kill us," Stregoni replied. "I won't be able to use my hand properly for weeks, possibly months – and it's not your fault your mother is dead! I won't simply stand by and let you believe that."

"What?" Aubrey said, the same time as his father. "Your mother died in childbirth, didn't she, Gille?"

Gille said nothing, merely folded his arms across his chest and stared coldly at the table.

"So that is what he has been holding over you," Sangre said softly. "I should have thought of it, but it seems so stupid. Gille."

Slowly Gille looked up, anger and humiliation and fear in his face, and Aubrey had never seen his cousin so...fallen apart.

"Gille, that is not your fault. My brother was cruel to convince you of such. If anything, I sense he really blames himself. Your mother was weak in body, did you know that? She was not much stronger than Carmilla. A childhood illness nearly took her life, and she never completely recovered. She made up for it in spirit...but she was warned that having children would likely be the death of her. Your father knew that. They took the risk anyway. It was not your fault."

Silence fell as Sangre finished speaking, and he and Gille stared at each other for a long time.

Then, without a word, Gille stood up and slowly left the room.

Stregoni sighed softly. "I think you did more good than I ever could have," he said. "Thank you."

Sangre shook his head. "I cannot believe all this time..." He sighed. "My arrangement with my brother was simple – I would take Gille, assume control of all his finances and such, and in return I would keep him well supplied and cared for."

"Well supplied?" Aubrey asked. "Well supplied with what?"

"Whatever drug he was taking," Stregoni guessed.

Sangre nodded. "Coca powder, to put a name to it. I thought the arrangement would save Gille and keep my foolish brother from causing further harm. I did not know he was manipulating Gille is such horrid fashion. I should have." He bowed his head, heaving a long sigh.

"That's not all he was telling Gille," Stregoni said, and tersely explained all that had transpired when he went to find Gille.

When he finished, Aubrey could not think of a single thing to say. Suddenly his cousin's behavior made a lot more sense. "Poor Gille," he said finally. "At least you are both safe now."

"Unless he comes after us," Stregoni said, shivering.

"I will take care of my brother," Sangre said. "Like I should have done a long time ago. It seems I keep making mistakes."

Aubrey shook his head. "He's your brother, father. I would have tried to tuck him away too – and who would ever imagine a man could be so cruel to his own son? The worst you ever do is start shouting, or go all icy."

Sangre looked at him briefly in amusement, but the troubled look returned too soon to his face. "Be that as it may, George will now have to be more harshly dealt with – I will not tolerate him hurting my children, and Gille has long been more mine than his." He looked at Stregoni's hand. "The Benefici family has always been more an extension of our family than mere friends. So, yes, my brother will be dealt with, even if I must take the most extreme of measures. I—"

A knock at the door stopped him, and Sangre called for the knocker to enter.

The maid who entered curtsied, then said, "My lord, the mistress has woken."

"Thank you," Sangre said, then sighed softly as the maid vanished again. "One unhappy moment after another," he said tiredly. "Brey, if you would like to see your sister, do so. Then she and I must have a talk."

Aubrey frowned, confused, but did not argue. Instead, he nodded and stood. "Stregoni, you should get some rest before you fall over."

Stregoni smiled faintly. "I believe I will, unless you need me to tend to Milla?"

"No," Sangre said. "There is nothing you can do for her. Go find Gille, for I sense he needs you very much right now."

"All right. I'll treat my hand and then go find him. Go see your sister, Brey."

Aubrey clasped his shoulder briefly in comfort, then preceded his father to the door, leading the way up the stairs – and realized Ruthven had followed him.

Carmilla was sitting up in bed when they arrived, still looking pale and sickly, but the slightest bit better than she had only a little while ago. "Brey," she greeted with a weary, but warm, smile.

"Milla," Aubrey said quietly, lightly touching her hand. "I'm glad you're awake."

"Me too," Carmilla replied, laughing weakly, clasping his hand. "I'm sorry to have had you all so worried."

Aubrey shook his head. "It's not your fault."

She smiled again, and started to speak, but paused when another shadow fell across the bed. "Papa," she said softly.

"Milla," Sangre said. "I am happy to see you awake." He turned to Aubrey. "If you will excuse us briefly, Brey."

"No," Milla said, as Aubrey stood up and Sangre took his place, perching beside her on the bed. She reached out and took his hands, squeezing them. "It's okay, papa. Brey can stay. Easier to say it once, than twice."

Sangre looked at her. "You already know."

"There were little things," Carmilla said, smiling, but she was blinking away tears. "It did seem awfully strange, papa, that I got so sick at the same time as Francois, when no one else n the house was affected. Combined with all the other little things..."

"Oh, angel, I am sorry," Sangre said, voice thick and heavy, as though some great weight held him down. He lifted her hands and kissed the back of them.

"It's okay, papa," Carmilla said quietly. "I'm sorry you've had to worry so much about me all these years."

Aubrey stared at them, feeling stupid and confused. "What am I missing?"

Ruthven looked at him. "She is only your half-sister, master. Her mother was not yours, but..."

"Mina," Sangre said, reaching out to gently brush away a stray curl of Carmilla's hair, not taking his eyes off his daughter. "We left the city for two reasons – we were tired of the rumors chasing us all over. The three of us were unorthodox, to be certain, but we loved each other deeply and wanted only to be happy together. Out here in the country, we did not have to put up so much pretense. We could be ourselves, and live freely and all as equals.

"The other reason," he continued softly, "was that Mina began to show signs of being in a delicate way."

Aubrey gaped. "But—Pets are rendered incapable of breeding."

"Yes," Sangre said. "Apparently, Mina was missed or it simply did not work properly. We never knew. But shortly after you were born, Brey, Mina gave birth to Carmilla. You are actually only a few months apart in age."

Aubrey sat down on the bed. "Huh," was all he could manage.

"So what now, papa?" Carmilla asked, wiping away the tears that had fallen down her cheek. "I've gotten way too sick this time, that's the only reason you'd finally tell me."

"I'm sorry," Sangre said softly, reaching out to embrace her. "I wanted only for you to be happy, and for no one to cause you any harm. It has terrified me from the moment you were born that someone would discover your true nature, and take you from me, one way or another. Your mothers worried constantly about you, though they were ecstatic to have a little girl they could dress up and someday take shopping and all manner of things."

Carmilla nodded, though her face was still buried against his chest.

Aubrey frowned in thought. "So, we need to find her someone whose blood she can drink." He scowled. "I'm not letting my sister become anyone's Pet."

Ruthven looked at him in amusement. "I do not think, master, that your family is the kind who will ever be Pet to anyone."

"I guess you would know," Aubrey replied tartly, "seeing as you make a poor Pet yourself."

Chuckling, Ruthven bent down to kiss him briefly.

Aubrey flushed. "Not here, you damned troublemaker."

"Yes, master," Ruthven replied, and rose to his full height. "If you will permit me," he said after a moment, "I might be able to solve the problem, at least to some degree."

They all turned to look at him.

"What are you talking about Ruthven?" Aubrey asked. "Have you got another one of your odd tricks?"

Ruthven merely smirked, then sketched Lord Sangre and Carmilla a deep bow. "If you will permit me," he said again, "I can at least ensure she is not ever bound to one person."

"That's impossible," Lord Sangre said, not releasing his daughter.

"No," Ruthven said softly, "it is not. Please."

Aubrey thought his father would protest, but after a moment Sangre stood up and moved aside.

Ruthven took his place alongside Carmilla. "I am certain this is more than a little unsettling for you, my lady, but I promise all will be well. All right?"

Carmilla nodded slowly, but reached out to clasp her father's hand.

Smiling gently, Ruthven lifted his wrist to his own mouth and bit down sharply. Blood trailed down it, dripping over his arm to fall on the bed sheets. He held his bleeding wrist out. "Now drink, but slowly, my lady."

She hesitated, but at an encouraging look from Sangre, finally swallowed nervously and accepted Ruthven's wrist, covering the slight wound with her mouth. Her eyes widened in shock, then slowly slid closed.

"Good," Ruthven said softly. Aubrey looked over his shoulder, unable to look away from the sight of his sister feeding like a Pet.

His sister was half vampire. It left him reeling.

After a few minutes, Ruthven said, "enough," and pulled his wrist away, lapping at the wound until it sealed.

Carmilla blinked sleepily at them, then her eyes fell shut, and stayed that way. Ruthven moved away as Sangre stepped forward to settle her more comfortably, smoothing the blankets and her hair for several long, agonizing minutes.

"Will she be all right?" Aubrey asked, when he could no longer bear the silence.

"Quite all right," Ruthven said, idly lapping at the drying blood on his arm. "My blood was the best possible way for her to start. She has gone her entire life without feeding properly, so starting with vampire blood is good for her. My body has already processed the blood, and her body can now learn how to do it properly. In addition to that, my blood type can accept all blood types. So," he smiled, "she will never be anyone's Pet."

Aubrey glared at him. "What in the hell are you?"

Ruthven smiled, looking like a particularly lazy and satisfied cat. "Only yours, master."

"Blood types," Sangre said. "You just mentioned blood types. Is that actually true, and how the hell do you know such a thing?"

"Perhaps we should discuss this elsewhere," Ruthven said, "and let the lady sleep."

"My study, now," Sangre snapped, and did not wait for a reply, but stalked from the room.

Aubrey looked at his Pet, but only shook his head, and led the way from the room.

In his father's study, he took one of the chairs in front of the desk, motioning for Ruthven to take the other.

"So tell me," Sangre said, "what you are, and why you know so much."

"I am nothing," Ruthven said, "save a Pet who knows more than he should."

Sangre glared at him. "I do not buy that for a moment – not when I hear how you saved Gille's life, and not with all you have just said."

Ruthven shrugged. "Whatever I may have been, I am that no longer. I belong to Aubrey, that is all."

Aubrey spoke before his father lost his temper. "So what's this about blood types? You speak of them as though it is known fact, when only days ago my father said it was merely a highly contested theory."

"It is forgotten," Ruthven said softly. "Vampires are born, you might say, with a blank canvas, so far as blood is concerned. That is why we can survive on animal blood, though it keeps us in a weakened state. What we truly crave and require is human blood, but once the blood of a human is tasted, that blank canvas takes on the image, if you will, of that first taste. After that, only a matching blood will suffice – the body ceases being able to tolerate any other type. Except..."

"Except what?" Aubrey asked when Ruthven fell silent.

"There are two very special types of blood. One is what you might call a free feeder – meaning any vampire can drink it, no matter what his personal type might be. The other, my type, is a free drinker. It means I can feed upon whomever I want, without any sort of difficulty."

Aubrey frowned. "Wouldn't it make more sense, then, to ensure that all vampires are free drinkers?"

"That was how it was done, once," Ruthven said softly. "Problems arose."

Sangre looked at him. "What are you?"

"Aubrey's Pet," Ruthven replied. "That is all, and my answer will never change."

"Why?" Aubrey asked. "It's obvious you don't need me."

Ruthven smiled at him in a way that made Aubrey's heart speed up. "On the contrary, master, I need you quite badly."

Aubrey felt his cheeks heat, but said nothing, merely subsided into silence.

He was stirred from his reverie as Ruthven abruptly stood up.

"Where are you going?" Sangre demanded, as Ruthven headed for the door.

Ruthven bared his teeth in a feral smile. "Your daughter will wake soon," he said. "I am going to find her a proper meal. Shall I feed her William, or your brother? Or fetch them both, and let her decide?"

Aubrey shivered, to see Ruthven look so. If he had ever played at being mild and submissive, no sign of it remained. He stood up and moved toward Ruthven. "Why would you do all this?" he asked, staring up into Ruthven's dark eyes.

"Because I want to," Ruthven said, "and it has been a long time since I have wanted anything. Do you want to join me in the hunt? I think William would make a better meal, hmm?"

"You know where William is?" Aubrey asked.

Ruthven shook his head. "No, not exactly, but he will not be hard to find."

"Then let's go find him, though I think my sister deserves something better than that."

Ruthven smiled again, and Aubrey though of wild animals – wolves and feral cats, or a circling hawk. "Revenge, master, often has a sweet taste. I assure you, she will not complain." He turned and bowed to Sangre. "My lord."

Farewell given, he turned and strode out.

Waving at his father, wondering what the hell was going to happen next, Aubrey followed him out.

Persimmon

(chapter seventeen)

Despite Gille's declaration, Stregoni was not certain he was supposed to be here. Every other time he had come to this room, there had been some silent, tacitly understood invitation between them.

He hovered in the doorway, uncertain.

Gille played like a man possessed, head bent over the keys as his hands moved effortlessly, drawing out a melody that expressed more clearly than words how Gille was feeling.

How long had he wanted the cold, hard Gille to fracture?

Now that he had, Stregoni hated it. Gille had obviously had his reasons and Stregoni hated to see him so torn apart.

Still not certain his presence was desired, he nevertheless ventured into the music room. If Gille did not want him here, he would make it plain.

Slowly he approached the piano, standing for a moment just behind Gille, watching him play, letting the music strike him, drowned out the pounding of his own heart.

Finally he sat down on one corner of the wide bench, facing away from Gille, his back just barely brushing against Gille's back and shoulder.

If Gille noticed, he gave no indication.

How long they sat that way, Stregoni did not know. Eventually, he closed his eyes and simply listened, felt, content to be simply a presence while Gille played and played.

He did not notice when the music stopped, not until an arm slid around his waist, and Gille nuzzled against his throat, breaths warm and still carrying a hint of laudanum and brandy. "Carrot..."

Stregoni swallowed, struck hard at the way Gille said that now. None of the coldness or mockery remained. He reached up and back, determined to touch in his own right – but Gille's hand caught his forearm.

"Your hand, idiot," Gille said quietly, but Stregoni could just barely hear the faintest thread of amusement.

He realized he had just tried to use his burned hand to touch Gille, and that would have hurt like hell. Smiling, he turned his head instead, meeting the green eyes. Tilting his head just so in invitation, he let his eyes fall shut as Gille kissed him, wishing fervently the remaining problems still hovering about would stay back for just a little while longer.

Gille abruptly pulled away, then Stregoni yelped as he was turned, lifted – and all but tossed down upon the chaise that called up so many hot, sweet, painful memories.

Stregoni blinked, then looked up, immediately recognizing the look in Gille's eyes. His blood began to heat, even as the doctor in him frowned with disapproval. "Gille, aren't you just a little too tired and strained for this nonsense? Aren't I?"

"Nonsense, Carrot?" Gille said, straddling him, then moving to rest his weight on hands and knees, long hair spilling over his shoulders to hide them both. "Is that what you call it? Clearly I have been doing something wrong all these years."

"I see you're recovering just fine," Stregoni muttered, yanking irritably at a strand of Gille's hair – then fisted his hand in it tightly as Gille nipped sharply at the skin just beneath his ear, making him gasp. "Bastard."

Gille did it again, and Stregoni would have hated him very much for going straight for the kill, but it felt too damned good.

"We should not be doing this," he said again. "You need rest, you mule-headed bloody bastard—stop doing that!" He let go of Gille's hair to thump his shoulder with his fist. "Gille, as much as I hate to turn down the offer, you—"

He thumped Gille again, but could not quite make himself break the kiss, the newness of Gille's kisses still too wonderful and devastating for him to muster the strength to refuse them. "Damn it, Gille," he said, the words turning into a long moan as a hand slipped beneath his shirt. "Why don't you ever bloody listen to me?"

"Defying you is more fun, Doctor," Gille replied.

Stregoni could see he was just avoiding the demons which had driven him to play only minutes before – but if it helped, then so be it. Maybe afterward the stubborn idiot would finally rest. If it were anyone else, Stregoni would just slip something in his tea or brandy.

With Gille, however...

Never.

Instead he simply decided to get revenge, good hand moving to the laces of Gille's shirt, then reaching up to take one nipple in his mouth—

A rough throat clearing made them both startle.

"What?" Gille snarled, levering himself up and turning around to glare at the servant stupid enough to intrude.

"Beg pardon, my lord," said the quaking maid. "Lord Aubrey isn't here, so I thought you'd be the next best one."

Stregoni slowly sat up, using Gille as leverage. "What's wrong?" he asked gently.

"His lordship's got a visitor, only we can hear them shouting something fierce, and glass breakin' and all, but he's locked the door and no one can get in."

Gille swore loudly and put himself to rights as they both stumbled from the settee.

"Thank you," Stregoni said, raking his hair from his face, sharing a look with Gille. "We'll take care of it."

"I've a spare key to his study," Gille said. "Upstairs." He did not waste any more time, but bolted from the room, taking the stairs two at a time and barreling down the hallway.

Stregoni didn't bother to go after him, but went to the library where he'd left his medical bag, then raced to the study just in time to meet Gille there.

Gille unlocked the door and threw open the door – then froze.

Moving around him, Stregoni immediately saw why he could not move.

Lord Sangre's study was a wreck – there was always some measure of clutter, for Sangre was a voracious reader and writer, but this...this was chaos. Paper everywhere, covering at least half the floor. Books strewn about, broken ink bottles, broken glasses and decanters. The entire room reeked of ink and brandy – and blood.

In the farthest corner of the room, two men were locked in struggle, as Sangre fought off the vicious attacks of his raging twin brother.

It was eerie, to see two Lord Sangre – one so well kept, elegant and refined, the other a mad mess, hurtling vile epithets as he attempted to assault his brother.

How long had this been going on? Had he been in the music room with Gille for so long? What in the hell had happened?

Dropping his medical bag, he moved across the room, grabbing up a heavy book on his way, using all the strength he could muster with one hand to slam it down on George's head.

It did not drop him, but it startled him enough to give Sangre the upperhand, and with a cry he threw his brother off. He slumped briefly against the bookshelves which lined two of his walls, meeting at the corner where the fighting had carried them.

"You are pathetic," he said scathingly to George, looking up just long enough to motion Stregoni back.

Obediently, he moved closer to the doorway, casting a wary look at Gille, who still had not moved, eyes on his father.

George heaved himself up – but Sangre was having none of it, and moved so quickly Stregoni barely followed the movement, face smashing into his brother's nose, and the smell of blood was stronger than ever.

Sangre kicked out, knocking his brother back to his knees, then grabbed him by the front of his shirt and shook him hard. "You're pathetic," he repeated. "The only smart and brave thing you ever did was to marry Ianthe, and it took my lovers to convince you to do it. You did not deserve it, but she loved you anyway, and died giving you a son – and this is what you do to thank her memory?"

Hurtling epithets and protests, George attempted to renew his attack – and Stregoni realized whatever sanity he'd had, it was now gone. Caused by the coca powder? Or simply the events of earlier?

Whatever the cause, Sangre granted him no pity, simply kicked his brother so that he was left gasping in pain.

And Stregoni could so easily see now in Sangre the man he must have been when he was younger – bold and brave enough to openly love two women, one of them a Pet, and to fight for the freedom a race that had so long been subjugated.

"You were pathetic as a child, and you are even more pathetic as a man," Sangre said in disgust, shoving his brother to the ground. "I cannot believe you would storm in here and cause so much discord—damn it."

He finally looked away from his brother, raking back his disordered hair, suddenly looking every bit his age. "Gille, you should not be here. Stregoni, take him away. I told the servants no one was to interfere."

Stregoni shook his head. "They were afraid for you, and came to find us."

Sangre grimaced. "I have been dealing with my brother all my life. I know each and every one of his nasty little tricks. There was no need for anyone else to get dragged into it. I will deal with him; take Gille away."

Nodding, Stregoni turned to do just that – but Gille chose that moment to step forward, walking slowly toward his father.

"Father—"

George looked up, hate and madness in his face. "You took her away," he said. "She wanted you so badly, and you killed her, and now you have taken away everyone else as well."

Gille flinched back, as though physically struck.

Stregoni yanked Gille back, stepping forward to stand between them. "Go to hell," he snarled. "Why couldn't you just stay in your own bloody house? It's not Gille's fault you're a fucking bastard. He didn't kill anyone, and he's not responsible for everyone abandoning you either. Aren't you overlooking that you're the one who got your wife pregnant in the first place? That you're the one who traded your son for a powder?"

George snarled, and lobbed a fallen brass book end at him.

He held his arm up to block it, even as he tried to move out of the way, but it wound up striking him hard on the shoulder, making Stregoni falter.

Gille's hand wrapped around his arm, pulling him back – but it was too late. George began to move at a feverish pace, picking up whatever he could get his hands on, throwing it all, chasing the projectiles with cruel and nasty words.

Stregoni was reminded suddenly of his own loss of temper, in Gille's room only a couple of days ago, and felt immediately ashamed and contrite. It must have upset Gille more than he would ever admit, and not knowing was no excuse – he would not let it be.

"I've had enough," Sangre said, and Stregoni saw his mouth move more than he actually heard the words, nearly everything drowned out by the screams and shouts coming from George, who approached them relentlessly.

They should run, Stregoni thought, but feared what would happen if George began to run amuck through the whole house.

From the corner of his eye he saw Sangre at the desk, saw him bend to pull something from a drawer – and at the last moment, saw what it was he held.

Turning, he shoved Gille down and covered his face, not wanting him to see—

The sound of the pistol shot was deafening in the small room, the sharp odor of gunpowder mixing unpleasantly with the tang of blood.

He looked up, horrified, first at Sangre, then at George, who lay unmoving by the fire. Blood spread out beneath him in a growing pool, lurid red against the tile of the fireplace and the deep jewel tons of the costly rugs, staining loose sheaves of paper and ruined books.

Swallowing, he looked back at Sangre. "You—Lord Sangre—"

"I should have done it a long time ago," Sangre said tiredly, sitting down heavily in his chair, covering his eyes with his hand. "Time and again, I fail to protect those who mean the most to me."

Stregoni did not release the hold he was barely maintaining on Gille. "Your children love you, and they're still alive."

Sangre laughed bitterly. "Indeed. Bloody hell, what a mess this has all become."

"Let me go!" Gille snarled, and finally succeeded in breaking free, shoving Stregoni away to regain his feet.

He stared pale faced at his dead father.

"I am sorry, Gille," Sangre said gently. "I had to choose – his life or yours. There was no contest."

Gille did not look away from the body as he spoke. "He was your brother."

"Not by our choosing," Sangre said wearily. "Anyway, you may as well be my son. My children are more important to me than anything. Still, I had hoped you would not see this – that is why my damned servants were told not to interfere." He slammed his hand down on his desk as he spoke, and then bellowed for the butler.

When the butler appeared, Sangre proceeded to tear him apart.

Stregoni barely heard the words, far more interested in Gille. Twining their hands together, he reached up with his burned one and gently turned Gille's head away from the grisly sight by the fireplace. "Gille."

Gille shuddered, turning his face into Stregoni's hand– then realized which hand it was, and immediately pulled away.

"Carrot, I think I'm ready to rest now." He looked at the body again, as though unable to help it. "He really did hate me, didn't he?" he asked softly.

"No," Stregoni said. "He hated himself, but was not willing to admit it."

Gille nodded, though it was clear he did not believe the words.

Stregoni suspected it would be many years before Gille would believe them – but at least he was listening, and allowed Stregoni to lead him from the study and up to his bedroom.

Pushing Gille back on the bed, he started to kneel to remove his boots – but Gille grabbed him and dragged him onto the bed, then removed his own boots and Stregoni's. "You can't do that with your hand, idiot. When are you going to remember it's injured?"

Rolling his eyes, too bemused by the fact he was in Gille's bed and Gille had put him there, Stregoni settled for lying back against the pillows and pulling Gille down to lie alongside him. "Go to sleep, idiot."

For once, Gille did as he was told.

Pink Verbena

(chapter eighteen)

"I don't understand what we're doing," Aubrey said, shivering in the cold.

Ruthven smiled in the moonlight, looking around the barren street where they lurked as though they stood in a warm, well-lit parlor room. "Waiting," he said.

"For what?" Aubrey said.

"Patience, master," Ruthven said, smile fading away as he frowned. "This is delicate work."

Aubrey looked at him, exasperated. "What is delicate work? Standing? Freezing?"

Ruthven laughed briefly, and held out one gloved hand. "Come here, master. I could use a taste, and you may take all of my warmth you like."

Grumbling half-hearted protests about confounding Pets, Aubrey took the hand and let Ruthven drag him close.

They had been wandering the town nearly all day, going back and forth across various streets and thoroughfares and alleyways. Six times Ruthven had stopped to feed – once on him, five times on others, and Aubrey had nearly suffered apoplexy the first time he did, and not been much calmer the subsequent four times.

Being told Ruthven could feed where he chose was one thing. Seeing it was quite another.

"Why are you feeding so much?" he demanded, even as he obligingly titled his head to bare his neck. When had he grown so complacent about this? When had he stopped minding the pain?

Ruthven hummed against his throat, arms tight around him, and Aubrey could do nothing but relax in his embrace.

"I am feeding excessively because I am using a great deal of my power to hunt out William," Ruthven said when he'd finished feeding.

"Power?" Aubrey echoed, the loss of blood and Ruthven's warmth conspiring to make him rather sleepy. "What powers?"

Ruthven laughed softly and kissed his temple. "Nothing, master."

"Don't 'nothing, master' me," Aubrey snapped, shaking off his sleepiness to look up and glare. "What are you – no, don't say my Pet. Better question – what *were* you before you became my Pet?"

"Nothing that matters now, master," Ruthven said, brushing his lips with a soft kiss. "I am yours, is that not good enough?"

Aubrey shook his head. "No, it's not. It makes no sense. There's nothing special about me. It's obvious you're powerful, whatever you really are, so why me?"

Ruthven sighed softly, and cupped Aubrey's face in his hands. They were little more than shadow in the moonlight, but he could still see enough of Ruthven's face to be entranced. He looked good in the moonlight, and despite the impossibility of it, Aubrey swore he could see his eyes as clear as day.

They were, as Ruthven had said, both all colors, and none.

"The first time I saw you, master, I woke up."

Aubrey frowned. "What?"

"I'd felt asleep for so very long, with no real reason to bestir myself. I saw you, and began to wake."

"Right," Aubrey said disbelievingly. "You saw me angry and displeased to be saddled with a Pet, unkempt from hard travel, and woke up from a very long sleep. Do I look like an idiot to you?"

Ruthven laughed. "That was not the first time I saw you, master. Indeed, I saw you many times before that night."

"What!" Aubrey glared. "You—"

"Quiet," Ruthven said abruptly, letting him go and stepping away. "I have found him."

Aubrey quelled an urge to stamp his foot, settling instead for silently cursing Ruthven. He started to speak, but Ruthven held up a hand, emphasizing he be silent.

It was so very like Ruthven to say something mysterious, then abruptly switch subjects.

"What are you doing?" he asked, when he could no longer endure the silence.

Ruthven frowned. "Calling him."

Aubrey opened his mouth to ask what the hell that meant, then changed his mind and simply gave up.

"A resister," Ruthven said quietly. "I have not encountered one of those in a long time." He grimaced and pressed his fingers to his temples, bowing his head as his eyes slid shut.

Frowning in concern, wanting to speak but remembering the repeated admonitions to silence, Aubrey settled for sitting down on a nearby bench. Crossing his arms, he scowled at Ruthven and waited for answers.

If anyone else had seen him thus, they would have said he looked exactly like his father.

He was stirred from his scowling by the sound of footsteps. He stood, wondering what other manner of maniac would be traipsing about the town at such an unholy hour of the night.

When he realized who it was walking toward them, he barely kept back a startled oath of surprise.

William. William was walking toward them – though there was something strange about his movements.

"Now I have you," Ruthven murmured, so low Aubrey almost didn't hear him.

He shot Ruthven an odd look, but Ruthven still had his eyes closed.

So he settled for watching William, who made him think of a sleep walker.

At last he reached them, stopping abruptly in front of Ruthven, who finally opened his eyes.

"Good little prey," Ruthven murmured.

Then he suddenly stepped forward, grabbed Williams hard, yanked his head to the side – and sank his fangs into William's throat.

"Hey!" Aubrey said, confused and hurt and – goddamn it all – jealous. It had been bad enough to watch Ruthven take his sustenance from others all day, but to see him feed upon the bastard who had caused his family so much harm.

Ruthven pulled away, laughing as he licked blood from his lips. "You taste sweeter by far, master," he said, eyes glittering in the dark as he looked Aubrey. "This is a necessity, not a pleasure."

"Shut up," Aubrey said, crossing his arms across his chest. "What are you doing?"

"Ensuring his obedience. It's much easier to control someone upon whom I've fed. Whatever natural resistance he had, it's no longer enough. He is mine to do with as I please." He grasped William's chin, smirking when there was no resistance.

William, Aubrey thought, might as well be a doll. "What did you do?" he asked, feeling the slightest shiver of fear.

"He would have killed all of you, I think, if he'd been given a chance. The weakest are always the cruelest, in the end." A shadow passed over Ruthven's face, a deep sadness even the dark could not hide.

Aubrey reached out before he even realized what he was doing, resting a hand lightly on Ruthven's arm. "Ruthven."

"Come, master," Ruthven said, pulling gently away. "It is time to teach your sister how to feed properly."

Heaving a sigh, Aubrey went obediently along as Ruthven led them along the streets. He stayed well away from William, who trailed them like some sort of odd stray dog. Shuddering, he unconsciously moved closer to Ruthven.

"It's entirely too late to be travelling home," he said. "If you try to put me on a horse, I will fall off it." He yawned widely, exhaustion hitting him now that the strange matter of hunting down William seemed to be over.

"Well, William cannot ride either, the state he's in," Ruthven said. "We are taking a carriage back, and you can sleep on the way."

Aubrey drew to an abrupt halt in the street. "No," he said flatly. "I do not ride in carriages, and not even you can make me."

"You can ride, master," Ruthven said patiently.

"No."

Ruthven took his hand, and dragged him close, lowering his head to give Aubrey a kiss – and then nipped down hard on his lip, drawing blood, sucking and lapping and kissing until Aubrey moaned. "Come, master," he said finally.

Aubrey went, but only because protesting suddenly seemed to difficult.

Still he felt cold and anxious as they reached the carriage house, and Ruthven nudged a sleeping guard awake.

Hastily Aubrey stepped forward, requesting the carriage and horses before anyone realized there was a Pet going around giving orders.

"I'll ride on top," he said when it was at last ready.

Ruthven merely gave him a look, and helped William into the carriage before turning to Aubrey. "Master."

Aubrey shivered at the tone, the expression, the way not a trace of Ruthven's false subservience remained. Whatever Ruthven was, he had finally dropped the pretense of Pet entirely – except for that persistent 'master'. "I'm not doing it, Ruthven."

"Yes, master," Ruthven said, but Aubrey knew it wasn't an agreement.

Instead he was grabbed, lifted, and neatly shoved inside.

The panic set in immediately, but just as he was about to start battling his way out, a wave of lethargy struck him. He fell back into the carriage seat, opposite William, and slumped back in the corner.

He yawned, suddenly finding it too difficult to keep his eyes open.

"There, master," Ruthven's calm voice washed over him. "You're just fine."

"You..." Aubrey managed to open one eye, and looked at Ruthven, a suspicion growing in his head. "You're not...doing to me what you've done to him, are you?"

Ruthven's voice was soothing as he replied, "Of course not, master."

"Liar," Aubrey replied, and fell asleep to the sound of Ruthven's warm laughter.

When he woke, he immediately panicked, and threw himself out of the open carriage door – and right onto the steps of his home.

He jumped as a hand landed on his shoulder, whipping around to see it was only Ruthven.

"Master?"

"I'm fine," Aubrey said irritably. "You and I are doing to have a discussion about me conveniently asleep, later."

Ruthven grinned. "Yes, master."

"Bloody impertinent Pets," Aubrey said, rubbing his eyes tiredly. "What time is it?"

The question was answered by the butler, who answered the door in his night robe. "Just past one in the morning, my lord."

Aubrey drew to a halt in the main hall as he saw that the door to the library was open, and a great deal of light spilled from it – and he could hear conversation and laughing. "Why in the world is everyone awake at this hour?" He raked a hand through his hair. "Why am I awake at this hour?"

"Come, master," Ruthven said, taking his hand and gently tugging him toward the open door.

"Stop calling me that," Aubrey groused. "It's completely ridiculous."

Ruthven's laughing reply was lost in the rush of startled greetings from his father, Stregoni – and Carmilla, who came running toward them and threw herself into Aubrey's arms.

Aubrey held her tight, too stunned to do anything else. His sister had run. Her arms were tight around his neck – almost too tight.

She pulled away after a moment and kissed his cheek.

"Milla..." Aubrey looked at her in wonder. "You look...you look healthy."

Carmilla laughed and hugged him again, then stepped away and turned to Ruthven, grabbing his hand and lifting it, kissing his knuckles. "Thank you, Ruthven."

"The pleasure was mine, my lady," Ruthven said, and withdrew his hand. "I am glad to see you looking well."

"I've never felt like this," Carmilla replied, spinning excitedly, then surged forward to give Aubrey another hug, before she crossed the room to kiss her father's cheek, before once more taking her seat again.

Everyone was gathered there – his father, and Elisabeth beside him on a stool her head on his thigh. Gille and Stregoni had taken over the long sofa, and Carmilla sat in the armchair closest to the fire.

It looked, he thought, rather homey. He smiled, wishing briefly for a moment that his mother and Mina were here as well, but content in the end with the family he did have.

Carmilla resumed speaking, breaking into his odd bought of sentiment. "It's strange, being a vampire, or half, I suppose, but..." She fluttered one hand. "It's strange, but not in a bad way. Well, yet. I...father said..."

Ruthven smiled, and pulled William into the room.

Gille, who until then had been sitting quietly with an amused Stregoni, stood up. "Him! I should—"

"Sit," Ruthven said.

Aubrey looked at him when Gille obediently sat, looking abruptly dazed and a little sleepy. "We are discussing this later," he hissed. "I don't know how the hell you do that, but stop it."

"Yes, master," Ruthven murmured, obviously ignoring the order.

Aubrey rolled his eyes, and gave up. Shucking his cloak, coat, gloves, and hat, he all but threw them at the butler then stomped over to the bar, helping himself to the brandy. "How has everything been while we were gone?"

The room fell suddenly silent, and he paused with the snifter halfway to his mouth. "Bad question?"

"Not well," Stregoni said, and quietly explained all that had transpired.

"I'm sorry, father, Gille," Aubrey said when he had finished. "Very sorry, indeed."

Both men nodded, but said nothing.

"That saves me the trouble of hunting him down, I suppose," Ruthven said mildly, then turned to Carmilla. "My lady, new vampires are always excessively hungry when they first begin to feed. Normally this is not a problem, for they are mere babes at this stage, and babes do not eat as much as a full grown adult. They also learn young the right ways to feed, and when to stop, and many other things besides. You have not had the benefit of this education, though I am certain you have unwittingly learned a few things simply being around Pets your entire life."

Carmilla shrugged, looking nervous. "Are you certain this is a good idea? I..."

"You fed from me just fine," Ruthven said gently, reassuringly. "If you could not do it, you would have refused then."

She looked at William, who still stood unmoving, unaware, nearby, and wrinkled her nose. "Must I touch him? He killed Francois, and nearly killed Gille, and probably wanted to hurt you and Aubrey and papa and Elisabeth too."

Ruthven bared his teeth. "Which makes him ideal for practice. If you do something wrong, only he is hurt, rather than a family or friend."

Carmilla winced.

"My lady, you are a blood drinker," Ruthven said, voice still gentle and kind, but firm. "It is your nature to drink – I promise you will grow used to it." He yanked hard on William, who dropped obediently to his knees. "The most common practice is to feed from the wrist. This causes little pain, and is easy enough to fix should something go wrong. The throat is the best place to bite, but takes experience, control, for it leaves both sides vulnerable."

His eyes flashed briefly, hotly, to Aubrey, and then were back on Carmilla, cool as anything. "Now, then," he said, and picked up William's arm. "You should know instinctively the right place to bite. Let us see you do it."

Anxiety and a little bit of fear upon her face, Carmilla swallowed and at first did not move. But with a last look at Aubrey, who smiled, and another at her father, who gave a deep nod, she took William's wrist and bit down.

Her eyes widened, something clearly surprising her, then fell half-shut as she fed.

It was a look Aubrey had seen before on the faces of Pets – on the face of his own. Whatever William's personality and temperament, clearly his blood tasted good.

Carmilla broke away with a soft gasp a few minutes later.

"Close the wound," Ruthven murmured.

"Oh," Carmilla said, startled, cheeks flushing as she hesitated a moment, then closed her mouth around the wound again.

When she pulled away, the wound was healed.

"Good," Ruthven said. "You will make an excellent vampire."

Carmilla laughed shakily. "I hope so, because it seems to be what I am." She turned to look at her father again. "Papa, is this truly all right?"

"Of course it is, angel," Sangre said softly. "I loved your mother, how could I not love you? It's what you are, and though I fear for you, at least now you are healthy."

She nodded, wiped away a few nervous tears, then sat back in her seat, hands folded neatly in her lap.

Aubrey dropped down into another chair and took a sip of brandy. "So what is my healthy sister going to do with herself now, I wonder? Run wild through the city? Stalk the countryside for pretty farm boys to feast upon?"

"Brey!" Sangre said sharply, shooting him a quelling look. "That is quite enough."

Rolling his eyes, Aubrey hid a snicker behind another sip of brandy.

"Travelling sounds like fun," Carmilla said with a sigh. "I've never been anywhere but here, since I was so weak."

"If that is what you want," Sangre said gruffly, "I suppose it could be arranged. Lord knows I have learned the folly of trying to keep your damned brother in one place. If the two of you must go *gallivanting* then I will not stop you."

Aubrey could see what it cost him to say it, the pain brought by the thought of both his children going away.

He realized suddenly he did not want to go anywhere.

Lord knew he had enough driving him crazy with a non-Pet following him about and calling him 'master'.

"I think I've had more than enough wandering," he said, carefully not looking at his father, though he could feel the startled glance directed his way. " We could arrange a suitable escort for Milla, I'm certain. She certainly deserves a chance to see the world that was always closed to her before. It would have to be someone we could trust with her secret, though, and offhand I know of no one."

Ruthven spoke up, "I might be able to help with that, if you are willing to trust me."

Aubrey groaned. "I should have known. You have an answer for everything."

"I live to serve, master," Ruthven said, dipping his head and looking up through his lashes, in a way he had not done for quite a while now.

"You are still not fooling anyone," Aubrey replied tartly, refusing to be affected by the playful, taunting gesture. "How can you help us, this time?"

"Let me dispose of this one," Ruthven murmured, standing up and taking William's arm, all but dragging him out of the room.

Aubrey started to stand up. "What are you going to do with him?"

"Stay, master," Ruthven said. "He is no longer useful, so I am going to get rid of him. I think it best if I did it alone."

Chilled by the look in the dark, dark eyes, Aubrey obediently sat.

Silence fell as Ruthven departed.

"What in the hell is he?" Gille demanded. "He is no Pet. I've never seen a Pet, even the boldest, act like him."

Elisabeth stirred from where she had been half-dozing with her head on Sangre's thigh. Sitting up, she braced her arms on his thigh instead, and looked around the room. "He is the Consort, of course."

"The what?" Aubrey asked, startled.

"Darling," Sangre said gently, "that's just myth and folklore."

Elisabeth looked up at him, frowning. "He is," she insisted. "He is too much like the story not to be."

"Who, or what, is the consort?" Aubrey demanded.

"It's an old vampire tale," Sangre said, stroking Elisabeth's hair as she lay back down, slowly moving to gently rub the back of her neck with his fingers. "The oldest stories of the vampires say that they were ruled by a court of six – the Prince and his five Regents, one each for the five sections of the small territory given over to the vampires back when they were free, and growing in number. Back then, the stories go, the ruling vampires had...powers, for lack of a better word."

"What powers?" Aubrey asked sharply.

Sangre shrugged. "No book I've ever found states explicitly what they are, only that vampires possessed powers – magic, and for that were a terrifying source. Those that believe the myths say that's one of the reasons people came to fear vampires, and decided to destroy or enslave them."

"And the Prince agreed," Elisabeth said softly, her voice taking on the tone of someone who is reciting something heard and said a thousand times, "because he loathed his own existence, and hated his own nature. Many of his people agreed with him...but many did not. It's said that many refused to accept such a fate, and rose up in protest."

"Yes," Sangre said. "The reality is probably only that he was assassinated, though there is no telling by whom, and of course the survivors chose slavery over death. The legend states, however, that a great crush of people rose up, refusing to die, and slew the Prince in his castle."

"They say the Regents defended him to the death, but they all died with him – save one, who was also the Prince's beloved, his Consort. They say he somehow survived, and escaped, and travels the world alone and ashamed."

Aubrey started to give his opinion on the utterly ridiculous tale when soft laughter from the doorway made him jump.

"No fair telling my story when I'm not in the room," Ruthven said, slowly stalking toward them, dark eyes sparkling. "Especially since you've got it all wrong." He stopped just behind Aubrey's chair, resting his hand lightly on the back of it. "I keep telling you I'm not what I used to be, and that's it's best left in the past, but humans never could leave well enough alone."

"Not when you keep being all strange and mysterious, no," Aubrey snapped. "So are you really this stupid legend I've just heard about? Why do vampires cling to it?"

"Any piece of the past is clung to, when it is all you have," Elisabeth said softly, and Aubrey immediately felt contrite. "The Prince wanted to kill us, as did his Regents. The Consort remains alive, and some say he has learned his lesson, for siding with the Prince...others say he merely waits to fulfill the wishes of his Prince." She looked at Ruthven. "Either way, he is not a vampire to anger."

Aubrey was suddenly reminded of the night he'd caught Ruthven in the hall with Elisabeth, the way she'd kissed his hand – out of fear? Respect? Why?

Ruthven laughed. "Side with the Prince! As if! Everyone says I defended the fool, when I'm the one who killed him, and in his own damned bed."

Marianthus

(chapter nineteen)

Aubrey tilted his head back, looking up at Ruthven, still behind him. "What in the hell are you talking about?"

Ruthven sighed, and looked down at him. "Five Regents, goes the legend, who chose to defend their lord and master at the cost of their own lives, simply so that he could wipe out all his people." His eyes flashed. "To hell with that. I have been alive for more than two hundred years, and I still do not believe my people are so despicable we deserve to be destroyed. Are humans any better? They do not drink blood, and they do not have my strange gifts – but they have other methods which can be just as cruel. No one wants to wipe them out."

He could think of nothing to say, taken aback by this bitterness he had never heard before.

Without even thinking, he reached up to touch Ruthven's cheek, soothed in his own way by the soft, warm skin. "Ruthven."

Strangely, Ruthven seemed startled by the touch. He reached up to capture Aubrey's hand, as though afraid Aubrey would change his mind and withdrew. He kissed the palm, then continued speaking.

"He told us his decision, that night over dinner, and could not understand why the five of us were so angry – I think he believed we really would follow him blindly. But unlike him, we were not ashamed of what we were. We spent more time in the real world than he, tending to the problems across the country while he stayed in his castle and bemoaned his fate." His lip curled in contempt. "I was his lover, it was true, but when we became lovers he was quite different. At that point in time, we were growing apart, and I was not terribly sorry for it. It was around that time people had taken to calling me the Consort, and it amused him enough to let the title stand."

"I cannot believe you're more than two hundred years old," Aubrey murmured. "How is that possible?"

"There were ten of us, at the start, who had the power and the longevity. Two killed themselves, for reasons long since lost. Two others were slain. Those four were reclusive. Six of us chose to stand in the light, and rule, and accept the risks that brought. The one they eventually began to call the Prince started out a fine leader, but he let the words of humans get to him, convince him he was a monster, and nothing we said could change his mind. He believed it so much, the people began to believe it – or at least many of them did. Even our powers could not sway their minds."

Ruthven sighed, looking down at Aubrey again. "The agreement was all but made, and we decided it was not to be bourn. So I waited until we went to bed, and let him have his way with me, and when he was sated and asleep I fed upon him. By the time he woke enough to realize something was wrong, it was too late to do more than struggle feebly. That's why my eyes the way they are, you know."

"They're like that because you killed him?" Aubrey asked.

"Because I fed upon one of my own," Ruthven said. "It's a stigma, or was, once. It's not unlike cannibalism, after all. I took his blood, his life, and gained all his power in addition to what I already possessed – it was the best and surest way to kill him, but I took no pleasure in it. No vampire that knew my eyes would have anything to do with me, save those four who stood with me, and knew my intentions that night."

Aubrey freed his hand and sat up just enough to turn around in his seat, frowning in confusion. "They're dead now, though, right? The other Regents?"

Ruthven laughed. "Hardly. After I killed him, Tepes stepped forward to assume control, and said we chose enslavement over death. Not long after that, the five of us made certain we were largely forgotten, and scattered to the winds. We have traveled since, always keeping an eye on our people, ensuring that we are as well as we can be."

"There's four more of you out there?" Aubrey demanded.

"Yes, master," Ruthven replied, laughing again. "It is one of them whom I thought would be able to play escort to your sister. I believe Varney is not too far from here."

Sangre snorted. "If you think I am letting my daughter roam foreign lands alone with a vampire who is probably at least as wily as you—I have more sense than that, thank you."

Ruthven grinned. "He would bring suitable female companionship, of course. She would be properly chaperoned." He paused a moment. "There would be no challenge otherwise?"

"I am not amused," Sangre said darkly.

"Oh, please, papa," Carmilla pleaded. "Ruthven would never do anything to hurt Aubrey, which means he would never harm me. Look at all he's done for us. Please, papa?"

Sangre heaved an aggrieved sigh.

"I think she will be safe enough, darling," Elisabeth said, smiling at Carmilla, then looking up at Sangre. "Come now, you are hardly one to moralize."

"I damn well am when it's my daughter," Sangre growled, but sat back in defeat. "Fine," he said, "summon your friend. But if he does not meet with my approval, this entire ridiculous affair is over." He pointed at Ruthven. "You are a born troublemaker."

Ruthven smiled. "So I oft am told, though this is the most trouble I've caused in decades."

Aubrey shook his head. "You cannot truly be that old. It makes even less sense that you are here – I do not believe for a moment that Gille picked you out. Why are you here?"

The levity on Ruthven's face faded, replaced by a terrible sadness. "A little over a decade ago, I heard many rumors about three people who were making great gains in the freeing of Pets. We dare not let it happen, and so I set out to persuade the three to quiet their efforts. I wanted to explain to them why we had done what we had, and why it should remain so, at least for the time being."

He looked at Sangre. "I arrived too late. The day I arrived here, a funeral was taking place for two of the three with whom I'd wanted to speak."

Sangre's eyes widened. "I remember—but I have never recalled your face before. You said you were a supporter, who had only recently arrived in town, and was sorry to have arrived at so awful a time. Why have I never remembered all of this before?"

Ruthven looked away, his eyes landing on Aubrey. "I have been alive a long time, and done things in that time that will never cease to haunt me. The Prince was not the only vampire I killed, nor the only one I fed upon. There will probably be others, for it is my duty to help control the Pets, until three hundred years have passed and the arrangement can be renegotiated. That day, after I spoke with your father, I saw you. You were a very pretty child, Brey, and quite sweet." He smirked. "I guess the temper came later."

"Che," Sangre said, but said nothing more when Aubrey glared at him.

"You made me smile, and that was something I had not done in longer than I cared to count. I left a few days later, but always kept tabs on your family. More than once, during my work, I saw you in a bookshop, or a café, or racing down the street to your classes." He smiled. "When I learned by chance, checking on the Pets still waiting to be purchased, that someone was seeking a Pet for you...I could not resist the impulse, or did not. Every time I saw you, I woke just a little bit more. It's good to feel alive again, and you alone are the reason for that, master."

Aubrey could only stare.

"I think he's redder than your hair, Carrot," Gille said drolly.

"You be quiet," Aubrey hissed, turning redder still.

Sangre glowered. "If your friend is even half so smooth a talker, Carmilla is going nowhere."

Carmilla rolled her eyes, then giggled at her brother.

"Ruthven," he finally managed. He shook his head. "You really should just stop calling me master. Honestly."

"You are my master," Ruthven said, and kissed him briefly. "Are there any more questions, or may I be allowed to put the past where it belongs?"

"What are these powers you keep mentioning?" Sangre asked.

Ruthven grimaced. "Many and varied, and I seldom bother to use them anymore. I can manipulate minds, to some degree. The way I transferred blood from Aubrey to Gille is not something most vampires can do – it is harder than you might think. There are other things, most of them listed in the various myths. Using them requires a great deal of energy, and the only way to restore it is to rest – which you have seen me do twice now – or drink vast quantities of blood. I prefer not to use them."

"We are so talking about this 'manipulate minds' later," Aubrey muttered.

"Yes, master," Ruthven replied, smirking.

Aubrey made a face at him, then turned around and dropped back down into his seat. "So I have a two hundred year old vampire with magic powers for a Pet. Gille – you are never allowed to pick out Pets, again."

"Apparently I did not pick him," Gille said dryly. "Tell your Pet to stay out of my head."

"Where do your powers come from?" Stregoni asked.

Ruthven shrugged. "I could not say. There were ten of us, in the beginning, but I remember little of those early days. Our powers were never passed down, I could not say why. When the five us finally die, one way or the other, all the powers will die with us. I am not the only one who prefers not to use them. They have always been more burden than blessing."

"Intriguing," Sangre said pensively, then shook his head. "It is a matter for another day, however. At the moment, it is nearly three in the morning. I think it's long past time we all found our beds."

Stregoni yawned. "It sounds a fine plan to me. Anything requiring thought can wait until the morning. Coming, Gille?"

"If I must," Gille groused, but did not protest when Stregoni tugged him from the couch, and kept hold of his hand as they left the room.

Sangre held his arm out to Elisabeth, who gathered up her skirts and reached up to kiss his cheek. "Come, Carmilla, we will walk you to your room." He slowed as they passed Aubrey and Ruthven. "Thank you, Ruthven, for everything."

"My pleasure, my lord," Ruthven said, bowing his head. "Good night, to you both."

Aubrey smiled faintly. "Good night, father. Milla, Elisabeth, pleasant dreams."

A moment later he was left alone in the study with Ruthven. Yawning, he leaned his head back against the chair and closed his eyes, enjoying the warmth of the fire and the lingering scent of forget-me-nots that permeated the place, probably the remnants of someone's perfume.

He opened his eyes as arms slid around his waist, a weight settling on his lap. He looked down to see Ruthven's head in his lap, looking weary and somewhat sad.

"I'm sorry we pressed you," he said quietly. "I guess I should learn to keep my nosiness to myself."

Ruthven moved in a way that suggested he was trying to shrug. "It would have come up, eventually – if only because at some point it would have been noted that I'm not aging."

"So you'll be young when I get old?" Aubrey asked.

"That is a discussion for another time, master," Ruthven replied, "if that is all right with you."

"Of course," Aubrey said, yawning again. "I really don't want to think about anything, least of all the fact that I seem to be attached to a vampire who is over two hundred years old. It's positively...incomprehensible."

Ruthven looked up, dark eyes as unfathomable as ever. "Is it really so awful, master?"

"I never said you were awful," Aubrey snapped.

"Not in so many words. If I am a trial, I will go..."

"Of course you're a trial," Aubrey said, tugging at Ruthven's hair in irritation. "You play at being submissive and it drives me crazy. You call me master even though we both know I'm not. You're impertinent and bold and take entirely too many liberties when told expressly not, you're entirely too clever for anyone's peace of mind, least of all mine—" He coughed, throat suddenly going tight. "Of course you're a trial, and you thrill at being so. But the idea of you leaving is unbearable, so I guess I shall simply have to learn to deal with you."

Ruthven lowered his lashes, and looked up through them, the submissive gesture completely ruined by the satisfied smirk on his face. "I'm certain, master, that I could find ways to make my presence more bearable."

"I've no doubt you could," Aubrey muttered, refusing to look at him and give in. "You're such a brat."

Soft laughter washed over his cheek, tickled his ear, and Aubrey turned back to make it stop, even knowing what was coming – and could not muster even a token protest as Ruthven kissed him, but sank his hand into Ruthven's hair, holding tightly as he gave back as good as he got.

"I still don't understand why you call me master, of all people," he said when they finally broke apart, unable to reconcile all he'd learned about Ruthven with the fact that Ruthven so obviously wanted him.

Ruthven scraped his teeth across Aubrey's throat, making his shudder. "I killed my lover to save my people, and bear a stigma of which I will never be rid," Ruthven said. "I survived that night, but felt as though I were dead. Something about you made me feel like living again, master. "

He yelped in surprise as Ruthven grabbed him and hauled him down to the floor. "Though, it does not hurt that you take so well to the bites. You are well-suited, master, to a vampire's embrace."

"Whatever," Aubrey muttered, grabbing the lapels of Ruthven's jacket. "I really don't care about any embrace but yours, so shut up already, unless you really want to keep talking."

"I live to serve, master," Ruthven said, and did not give Aubrey a chance to voice his scathing reply.

Larkspur

(epilogue)

"Brey! Stop being such a lay-about!"

Aubrey opened one eye and scowled at his sister. "What's the bloody point of a picnic if I can't be insufferably lazy? You want to run around in this heat, by all means. I am staying right here to wallow in sloth."

"You!" Carmilla said, and kicked him lightly one last time before running off to play badminton with Elisabeth.

Soft chuckles from nearby stirred him just as he was slipping back into a light doze. "You are being awfully lazy today, master."

Aubrey turned to look at Ruthven, who was determined to make him commit yet another sin, dressed only in breeches that fit far too well, a white lawn shirt barely laced, and pale green collar embroidered with apples.

He closed his eyes again. "So says the man who kept me up all night."

"I did not hear any complaints," Ruthven said, more than a little smugness in his voice.

Aubrey did not deign to give him the satisfaction of a reply.

Instead he simply listened to his sister and Elisabeth, the occasionally called advice or gentle taunt from his father, the more distant voices of Gille and Stregoni, who had wandered away to go fishing, off all things.

"Is there any wine left?" he asked.

"Could you be bothered to get it if there was, master?" Ruthven asked.

Aubrey would have rolled his eyes, but that required opening them. "It is entirely too hot to be impertinent."

"I rather like the heat."

"You're insufferable."

Ruthven laughed, then fell silent.

Aubrey yawned and rolled over onto his stomach, wishing the shade offered by the tree they were beneath were a bit more expansive. He cracked his eyes open to look at Ruthven, flushing when he realized Ruthven had been staring at him all the while. "What?" he asked.

"The sunlight suits you, master," Ruthven said – then smirked. "Even if it does make you as lazy as a cat."

"Shut up," Aubrey muttered, and pointedly turned away to face the other way, watching Stregoni and Gille at the pond a little distance away. It looked as though they had about as much interest in fishing as he did in moving.

Snorting, he turned to face Ruthven again. "I might be as lazy as a cat," he said, "but you looked like you helped yourself to the mistress' canaries."

"Merely enjoying the view, master."

"Brat," Aubrey said, and closed his eyes again, too hot and sleepy to muster the energy for a sharper retort.

The sound of a footman's voice did stir him though, and he dragged himself to a sitting position as he watched the footman talk to his father.

A moment later, Sangre beckoned to him.

As he drew close, he realized that Carmilla looked too excited too contain herself.

"What is it, father?" he asked.

Sangre looked at Ruthven, who stared blandly back. "It would seem a sudden guest has arrived, claiming to be a friend of a certain Pet on the premises."

"Hmm," Ruthven said idly. "I did not expect him for a couple of days yet."

"Liar," Aubrey muttered beneath his breath, but was given no chance to say anything further as a man drew close, escorted by another footman.

No way, Aubrey decided, sharing a look with his father. No way in hell was he taking Carmilla anywhere – least of all out of their sight.

He had long blonde hair, pale enough it was almost white, neatly pulled back by a red silk ribbon. His waistcoat was also red, entirely too bright and flashy for Aubrey's taste. His eyes were a pale blue, almost more gray, really. He was also more than a little bit handsome – almost pretty, in fact, and at least as tall as Ruthven.

Carmilla, he decided, was staring inappropriately. Non too gently tugging his sister back, he stepped forward. "You are Ruthven's friend?"

"Yes," the man said, smiling in a way that showed he did, indeed, have fangs. "My name is Varney. It is an honor to meet all of you." He swept into a deep bow, then glanced up at Carmilla, holding out his hand. "I believe you are the fair princess I have been asked to show the world?"

Carmilla put her hand in his, cheeks going pink when he kissed her knuckles.

"Unhand my daughter at once," Sangre said sharply.

"Oh, papa," Carmilla said with a sigh. "Do not start growling."

"I will growl all I like," Sangre said.

Carmilla exchanged a look with Elisabeth, who placed a placating hand on his arm. "Dear, it's far too lovely a day to start picking fights." She looked at Varney. "You were, I believe, to bring a proper chaperone for her ladyship?"

"Yes, my lady," Varney replied. "She follows in a carriage, and should be arriving within the hour. She is, technically speaking, my master. I have been her Pet for twenty years. A very sweet woman, and you will be happy to know she relishes putting me in my place. Alas, she is far too good at it." He smiled, making Carmilla and Elisabeth laugh.

Aubrey shared another look with his father, and another with Gille as he and Stregoni at last joined them.

Before they could start in on the man, however, Elisabeth clapped her hands briskly. "Well, then, I say we all sit down and get to know one another in *civilized* fashion. Shall we return to the house, darling, or continue to enjoy the fine weather?"

"The weather," Sangre said, and gave her his arm to lead her back to the blanket, though he did not completely abandon glaring at Varney.

Who offered his arm to Carmilla.

Aubrey ignored the amused looks Ruthven was shooting him, and lead the way back to the three, and the large blanket upon which he'd been so recently napping.

From the warning glint in his sister's eye, he suspected they were going to lose the battle to keep her from going off with Varney and this supposed chaperone on her way – but they could have fun trying, and making certain the man was fit to take away his sister.

"Aren't you sitting just a little too close?" Gille demanded, glaring at Carmilla, who had chosen to sit next to her potential guide.

"No," Carmilla said airily. "No worse than you and Stregoni at the fishing hole."

"That was entirely different," Gille snapped.

Stregoni laughed and dragged the picnic basket close, coming up with a bottle of wine, which he quickly decanted, passing the glasses around until everyone had one. "Come now, it's bad for the health to bicker this early in the day. Just look at what it did to poor Aubrey – he cannot even stay awake."

Aubrey rolled his eyes, but obediently lifted his glass as Stregoni did.

"To new friends," Stregoni said, elbowing Gille to raise his own glass. "And best wishes to Carmilla, when she leaves on her travels."

"She's not going with him," said Aubrey, in unison with his father and Gille.

"Are they always like this?" Varney asked, amused.

"Always," said Carmilla, in unison with Elisabeth, Ruthven, and Stregoni.

Aubrey rolled his eyes, but laughed along with everyone else.

Fin

Lightning Source UK Ltd.
Milton Keynes UK
UKOW051548020812

196969UK00001B/27/P

9 781936 202034